How they came to be

QUANTUM MEN

Buried deep beneath an abandoned military base, in reinforced bunkers long ago forgotten by the outside world, a group of supersoldiers was born, a black ops team not only trained in combat, but also imbued with extraordinary skills that allow them to defy dimension, reality and time itself.

When a top secret mission goes terribly awry, three special heroes are forced to accept their own mortality. Abandoned and betrayed by ruthless superiors, they must struggle to put the pieces of their lives—and their memories—back together. But in resurrecting those memories, secrets will be uncovered. Lives will be lost. And a dark and deadly conspiracy will finally be exposed.

Dear Harlequin Intrigue Reader,

Take a very well-deserved break from Thanksgiving preparations and rejuvenate yourself with Harlequin Intrigue's tempting offerings this month!

To start off the festivities, Harper Allen brings you *Covert Cowboy*—the next riveting installment of COLORADO CONFIDENTIAL. Watch the sparks fly when a Native American secret agent teams up with the headstrong mother of his unborn child to catch a slippery criminal. Looking to live on the edge? Then enter the dark and somber HEARTSKEEP estate—with caution!—when Dani Sinclair brings you *The Second Sister*—the next book in her gothic trilogy.

The thrills don't stop there! *His Mysterious Ways* pairs a ruthless mercenary with a secretive seductress as they ward off evil forces. Don't miss this new series in Amanda Stevens's extraordinary QUANTUM MEN books. Join Mallory Kane for an action-packed story about a heroine who must turn to a tough-hearted FBI operative when she's targeted by a stalker in *Bodyguard/Husband*.

A homecoming unveils a deadly conspiracy in *Unmarked Man* by Darlene Scalera—the latest offering in our new theme promotion BACHELORS AT LARGE. And finally this month, 'tis the season for some spine-tingling suspense in *The Christmas Target* by Charlotte Douglas when a sexy cowboy cop must ride to the rescue as a twisted Santa sets his sights on a beautiful businesswoman.

So gather your loved ones all around and warm up by the fire with some steamy romantic suspense!

Enjoy,

Denise O'Sullivan
Senior Editor
Harlequin Intrigue

HIS MYSTERIOUS WAYS

AMANDA STEVENS

HARLEQUIN®

TORONTO • NEW YORK • LONDON
AMSTERDAM • PARIS • SYDNEY • HAMBURG
STOCKHOLM • ATHENS • TOKYO • MILAN • MADRID
PRAGUE • WARSAW • BUDAPEST • AUCKLAND

ISBN 0-373-22737-X

HIS MYSTERIOUS WAYS

Visit us at www.eHarlequin.com

Printed in U.S.A.

ABOUT THE AUTHOR

Amanda Stevens is the bestselling author of over thirty novels of romantic suspense. In addition to being a Romance Writers of America RITA® Award finalist, she is also the recipient of awards in Career Achievement in Romantic/Mystery and Career Achievement in Romantic/Suspense from *Romantic Times* magazine. She currently resides in Texas. To find out more about past, present and future projects, please visit her Web site at www.amandastevens.com.

Books by Amanda Stevens

HARLEQUIN INTRIGUE
373—STRANGER IN PARADISE
388—A BABY'S CRY
397—A MAN OF SECRETS
430—THE SECOND MRS. MALONE
453—THE HERO'S SON*
458—THE BROTHER'S WIFE*
462—THE LONG-LOST HEIR*
489—SOMEBODY'S BABY
511—LOVER, STRANGER
549—THE LITTLEST WITNESS**
553—SECRET ADMIRER**
557—FORBIDDEN LOVER**
581—THE BODYGUARD'S ASSIGNMENT
607—NIGHTTIME GUARDIAN
622—THE INNOCENT†
626—THE TEMPTED†
630—THE FORGIVEN†
650—SECRET SANCTUARY
700—CONFESSIONS OF THE HEART
737—HIS MYSTERIOUS WAYS††

*The Kingsley Baby
**Gallagher Justice
†Eden's Children
††Quantum Men

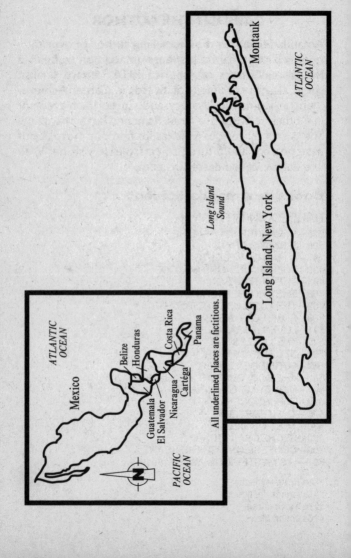

ATLANTIC
OCEAN

Montauk

Long Island
Sound

Long Island, New York

ATLANTIC
OCEAN

Mexico

Belize
Honduras

Costa Rica

Guatemala
El Salvador
Nicaragua
Cartéga
Panama

N

PACIFIC
OCEAN

All underlined places are fictitious.

CAST OF CHARACTERS

Melanie Stark—She's come to the tiny Central American country of Cartéga to find the one man who can unlock the secrets of her past.

Jon Lassiter—A ruthless mercenary known as *el guerrero del demonio*—the demon warrior.

Richard Stark—Once a quantum physicist for a top secret operation known as the Montauk Projects, he's been on the run for years.

Dr. Wilder—An American doctor involved in a very dangerous business.

Hoyt Kruger—He's hired *el guerrero del demonio* to protect his oil wells in Cartéga. But does he have an ulterior motive?

Martin Grace—Kruger's partner is a man of few words…and fewer scruples.

Angus Bond—An Australian expatriate with a fondness for the bottle and a penchant for trouble.

Blanca del Torrio—Is she really in love with Dr. Wilder, or does the older man have something she wants?

Chapter One

They called her Angel because they didn't know her real name and because the tiny hand-shaped birth-mark on the left side of her face made it seem as though she'd been touched by God.

Even so, she was a very sick child, the latest victim of a deadly epidemic that had swept through remote villages along the banks of the Salamá River in the tiny Central American country of Cartéga.

Melanie Stark had found the little girl on the steps of the clinic in Santa Elena when she'd gone there to volunteer. Huddled beneath a dirty, ragged blanket, the child had been suffering from high fever, chills, chest congestion, persistent cough and a florid maculopapular rash over her face, arms and trunk that was similar to, but not entirely consistent with typhus.

Where she had come from or who had left her, no one knew. For the first forty-eight hours, her condition had been touch-and-go. Finally, on the third day, her temperature had dropped and her breathing became less labored, but she still had a long way to go for a full recovery.

Melanie had barely left the little girl's bedside since she'd frantically carried her into the clinic three days ago. She'd sat with her morning and night, reading to her, talking to her softly, sometimes praying. Now she reached out to touch a tiny hand beneath the oxygen tent, but the child didn't stir.

Dr. Wilder, who ran the clinic, squeezed Melanie's shoulder, then nodded toward the door. Reluctantly, she got up and followed him out. His solemn expression alarmed her.

Melanie turned to him anxiously once they were outside the closed door. "She's better today, right? Her fever is down, her color is improving…"

"Yes, that's the good news." Dr. Wilder stripped off his surgical gloves and dropped them in a nearby waste receptacle. He wasn't a particularly tall man, standing only a couple of inches above Melanie's five foot seven, but he was trim and toned and the close-cropped beard and mustache gave him a distinguished, intellectual appearance. He was American, but Melanie couldn't place his accent.

When she'd first met him, she'd judged him to be around fifty-five, but after having spent the past few days in his company, she'd come to the conclusion that he was one of those men whose age could be anywhere from late forties to late sixties.

He was refined, gentle, a very good doctor from what she'd observed, although, admittedly, a premed dropout such as she was perhaps not the best judge.

Still, she'd been impressed with his care and treatment of Angel. Melanie was convinced the child wouldn't have made it through that first day without Dr. Wilder's expertise.

Why someone with his obvious skill and talent had ended up in a place like Santa Elena, she couldn't imagine. Nor did she ask. She'd learned a long time ago that curiosity courted curiosity. Her own reasons for coming to Cartéga were private and complicated—perhaps even dangerous—and she had no intention of discussing them with anyone, much less dragging an innocent bystander into her murky quest.

Dr. Wilder's worried gaze met hers. "Angel is responding to the treatment, but unfortunately, the epidemic has depleted our supply of antibiotics. I've made repeated calls to the Ministry of Health in San Cristóbal, but the government either can't or won't help us. I haven't even been able to get the results of Angel's blood tests, and without them, I can't even be sure what we're dealing with…"

He trailed off, shaking his head in disgust. "The minister claims that airlifted medical supplies from the U.S. are being stolen by the rebels, but I'm just as inclined to believe they're being confiscated by the army to sell on the black market."

If Melanie had learned anything in the brief time she'd spent in Cartéga it was that in the bloody civil war that had raged for nearly five years, there were no good guys. Only victims like Angel.

She drew a long breath. "What happens to Angel if we run out?"

Dr. Wilder glanced at the door behind which the tiny, dark-eyed girl valiantly fought for her life. "She's very weak. Without the antibiotics, her immune system may not be able to fight the infection. Complications could set in. Pneumonia, acute renal failure…" He gave a helpless shrug. "Without the drugs, she could die."

"We can't let that happen. I *won't* let that happen," Melanie said stubbornly.

He gave her a weary, defeated smile. "We may not have a choice. Some things are out of our hands. If the shipments can't get through…"

"We'll just have to find the drugs somewhere else."

He frowned. "Where?"

Melanie thought for a moment. "An American oil company has a drilling site thirty miles north of here at the base of the mountains. They have an infirmary on the premises, as well as an airstrip, and supplies are flown in twice a month."

Dr. Wilder's gaze narrowed. "How do you know that?"

"I talk to people in the village. I hear things," she replied evasively.

"Did you also hear that the drilling site is like a fortress?" Dr. Wilder demanded. "Kruger Petroleum has hired a small army to guard the perimeter of the compound. No one can get in or out without proper authorization. You won't get within a hundred yards before you'll be turned away."

She shrugged. "We'll see about that."

"Melanie…"

"Look, I'm not going to let that little girl die, Dr. Wilder, no matter what I have to do. But things could get a little dicey," she admitted. "The less you know the better off you'll be."

"Deniability, you mean."

"Exactly. But please don't worry. I know what I'm doing."

"I hope you do. Because I hear things, too." Dr. Wilder's expression turned grim, cautious. "The mercenaries Kruger has hired to guard his wells are a pack of ruthless savages, the kind who shoot first and ask questions later. They're led by a man the locals call *el guerrero del demonio.*"

Demon warrior.

An icy dread tingled down Melanie's backbone.

"They say he has…unnatural powers."

Melanie forced a smile to her suddenly frozen lips. "You're a man of science, Doctor. Surely you don't believe in superstitions."

"Where science is corrupted, evil often flourishes," he muttered obliquely. "Tread carefully, Melanie."

The hair at the back of her neck lifted at his strange warning, and she watched him curiously until he'd disappeared down the hallway. Then she turned and slipped through the door to Angel's room.

Resuming her position beside the child's bed, she settled in to await the coming darkness.

THUNDER MINGLED with gunfire in the mountains as nightfall swooped like a vampire's cloak over the jungle. Jon Lassiter scanned the area in the deepening twilight as a knot of tension formed in the pit of his stomach. It was a familiar sensation. A mixture of elation, dread and adrenaline that he always experienced before a battle.

Neither the storm nor the rebel skirmishes with the Cartégan army had moved any closer in the past twenty-four hours, but he wasn't about to let down his guard. He'd learned a long time ago that disaster usually struck when and where you least expected it.

And in Cartéga, disaster was never far away.

The tiny Central American country had once been little more than a blip on the international radar screen, a lush, primitive paradise that time and progress had forgotten. But the discovery of oil, along with one of the most significant archaeological finds in decades, had propelled Cartéga onto the world stage.

Representatives from all the major oil companies had stampeded into the sleepy capital of San Cristóbal, throwing enough money around to corrupt an already corrupt government. Lassiter had no idea how Kruger Petroleum, his current employer, had managed to outsmart the international conglomerates, but knowing Hoyt Kruger, it had probably been a combination of charm, chicanery and a pact with the devil.

Lassiter could appreciate that.

A chain-link fence topped by razor wire enclosed the compound, and sentries were posted at the en-

trance and at intervals around the perimeter. Lassiter
nodded to the dozen or so guards he encountered as
he made his nightly rounds. He didn't know half their
names, nor did he want to. He didn't trust any of
them. Money could buy a lot of things in this part
of the world, but seldom loyalty.

Lassiter could appreciate that, too. He was a member of a dark and sinister society whose allegiance
was sworn only to the highest bidder, and he labored
under no delusions about his men's fealty. He commanded this operation for one reason only. The
money came through him. In another time, another
country, in another hellhole of a jungle, he was just
as likely to be following the orders of one of his
comrades. Or to be fighting against them. It all depended on the price, and every man had one.

As he walked back inside the camp, Lassiter
breathed in the familiar fragrance of rotting vegetation, cigarette smoke, sweat and diesel fuel. And
fainter, the acrid smell of gunpowder that clung to
the twilight like the remnant of some mostly forgotten nightmare.

The past three years of his life were all wrapped
up in that smell, Lassiter thought with a keen sense
of inevitability. The location changed—Nicaragua,
Guatemala, El Salvador—but that scent stayed the
same. He sometimes thought he could smell it on his
skin. Like the stench of a rotting corpse, it had gotten
into his pores, his hair shafts, his sinuses. He could
no more scrub that odor away than he could banish
the screams from inside his head.

Screams from another life, one he only vaguely recalled, although at times the memories would come back with startling clarity, usually after one of the dreams. Then he'd lie awake, staring at the sky and forcing himself to recall everything he could about his previous life—the farm where he'd grown up deep in the Mississippi Delta, his frail mother, a girl named Sarah who'd wanted to marry him.

He had no idea what had happened to that girl. He didn't even know if his mother was still alive. Home was a lifetime away.

Stopping for a moment to light up one of the thin, black cigarettes he ordered from a cigar shop in Tegucigalpa, he listened to the raucous laughter and cursing coming from the crew as they continued to work in the illumination from the floodlights that had been set up around the third well site. They worked in twelve-hour shifts, just as Lassiter's men did.

When Kruger had first moved in the heavy equipment six months ago, preparing for what promised to be a long and profitable arrangement with the Cartégan government, he'd been assured of round-the-clock protection. But then the rebel incursions had intensified around the capital, and the beleaguered and poorly equipped army had been called into service to snuff out the guerrilla encampments in the mountains.

His operation soon the target of saboteurs and snipers, Hoyt Kruger had decided to put together his own army, not just as protection against the rebels, but as a safeguard in the event one of the local drug lords decided to move in and try to take control of the wells.

When word had reached Lassiter in Caracas that Kruger wanted to meet with him, he'd been a little surprised by the request. The reputation he'd acquired in Central America hadn't exactly served him in good stead in recent months. Clients had become few and far between, which was why he'd drifted south. But he'd had a feeling from the moment he shook Kruger's hand, sealing the deal, that the rumors keeping others at bay had been the reason the enigmatic Texas oilman had sought him out in the first place.

Lassiter ground the half-smoked cigarillo beneath his heel, then continued on his rounds. The camp consisted of five tin barracks crowded with bunks—four housing the drilling crew and one for Lassiter's men—an office packed with computers connected to Kruger's headquarters in Houston via satellite, a mess tent, a medical clinic and a rec hall of sorts where the off-duty crew could watch videos, play cards or shoot the bull. Not exactly the most effective activities for warding off tension and boredom, but on rotating weekends, there was the always unpredictable nightlife in Santa Elena, a thirty-minute jeep ride away.

The door to the office was open, and Lassiter could see the gleam of Kruger's bald head in the glow of a CRT screen as he and his partner, Martin Grace, pored over the paper scrolling out of the printer like cardiologists reading an EKG.

Kruger was tall and powerfully built, not handsome except for his piercing blue eyes. He was in his late fifties, a good twenty-five years older than Lassiter, but still with a quick mind, a quick temper and an uncanny knack for making money.

Sensing Lassiter's scrutiny, the two men looked up with tense expressions, then Kruger relaxed when he saw who it was. But Grace's features tightened. He didn't like Lassiter and made no bones about it.

He wasn't a small man, probably just shy of six feet, but Kruger seemed to dwarf him, in both stature and personality.

"Don't you know how to knock?" he barked irritably.

Lassiter shrugged. "Door was open."

The offhand remark seemed to irritate the man even more, and Kruger laughed. "You'll have to excuse Marty, Lassiter. He's been jumpy ever since he got here. But he'll soon get used to the gunfire, right?"

Lassiter shrugged. "I hardly even notice it."

Martin Grace's eyes narrowed. "Forgive me for pointing out the obvious, but isn't it your job to notice the gunfire? And what about the snipers?"

"What about them?"

"The men were fired on again yesterday. Luckily, there weren't any injuries, but that's no thanks to you. We hired you to protect the crew and our interests down here, but I'm starting to wonder if that's what you're doing."

Lassiter's name crackled over the radio fastened

to his belt, and he gave Martin Grace a pointed look. "We'll have to take this up later. I'll come look you up as soon as I take care of this matter."

Grace glanced down at the paper in his hand as if suddenly alarmed by the notion of a one-on-one meeting with Lassiter. "I've said my piece," he mumbled.

Lassiter nodded to Kruger, then stepped outside to answer the radio. Lifting the unit to his ear, he said his name into the transmitter.

"It's Tag," the man on the other end responded. "I've picked up something on one of the monitors you need to take a look at."

"What is it?"

Taglio hesitated. "I think you'd better see it for yourself."

Uneasiness tripped along Lassiter's nerve endings. There was something in Taglio's voice—

"Anything wrong?" Kruger stood in the doorway, one hand propped against the frame as he regarded Lassiter anxiously.

Lassiter shrugged as his gaze met the older man's in the semidarkness. "Whatever it is, I'll take care of it."

"See that you do. The men are getting skittish with all that damn gunfire. And I heard today a kid was brought into the clinic in Santa Elena with the fever. When the crew gets wind of that…" He didn't bother to finish the sentence, but Lassiter knew what he was thinking. The disease, along with the fighting, was getting closer.

Shouldering his rifle, Lassiter strode across the camp to the sheet-metal building that served as operation headquarters. As he neared the structure, the smell of diesel fuel from the generator grew stronger.

Part of the bargain Kruger had struck with the Cartégan government had been the routing of electrical lines through the jungle to the camp. But even in the capital, service was unpredictable at best, and Lassiter hadn't wanted to take a chance on a complete power blackout.

The generator was a safeguard and had been one of a long list of items he'd presented to Kruger before he'd signed on to the operation. To the oilman's credit, he hadn't batted an eye at the price tag. And with good reason, Lassiter figured. His fee for services and equipment was substantial, but the wells that had already been drilled were producing thousands of barrels a day. If they continued at that rate for several months, let alone years, Kruger Petroleum stood to make millions.

Along with the generator, Lassiter had also requested portable thermal-imaging cameras which he and his men had camouflaged and mounted around the perimeter of the camp. The monitors were watched around the clock in the event the guerrillas or one of the drug cartels—or even the Cartégan army—decided to launch an assault.

The door to the building was open to allow in the night air, and when Lassiter stepped inside, Taglio glanced up with a frown. He was several years younger than Lassiter, well educated, well traveled and with a grace and style that often caused people to underestimate his toughness. Sometimes even Lassiter wondered what had brought a man with Danny Taglio's looks and privileged background to a place like Cartéga, but he never asked. No one ever asked.

"You better take a look at this," the younger man said.

Lassiter crossed to the monitor and watched as Taglio played back one of the surveillance tapes. Noting the time and date in the right-hand corner of the screen, Lassiter automatically glanced at his watch. Less than five minutes had elapsed since the image he was now watching had been captured on tape.

"Which camera?" he asked.

"Sector Seven." The camp was divided into a grid similar to a tic-tac-toe board. Sector Seven was the lower left corner, the area closest to the mountains and to the heaviest guerrilla fighting.

Lassiter studied the screen. The resolution from the thermal-imaging cameras was a vast improvement over the night-vision equipment they'd once had to work with, but a thick mist had drifted down from the cloud forest, obliterating almost everything on the screen. Lassiter could make out the vague shape of trees, but that was about it. The camera spanned down, and the fence around the compound came into focus.

"I can't see a damn thing," he said. "What am I supposed to be looking at?"

"Just keep watching. It should be coming up—"

Taglio glanced at his own watch "—right about...
now."

Lassiter caught his breath. The image was there,
then gone in a single heartbeat. He couldn't even be
sure of what he'd seen.

"Roll it back."

Taglio did as he was instructed, and Lassiter
watched the monitor, not daring to blink. "Freeze
it!"

It took Taglio a couple of tries before he was able
to freeze the frame Lassiter wanted, but when he had
it, Lassiter leaned forward, a chill going through his
body. "What the hell?"

"It's a woman," Taglio said. "Right outside the
fence."

She wore a scarf over her head, but Lassiter didn't
think she was one of the local peasants. "Where'd
she come from?" he muttered. They were miles from
any kind of civilization.

"The better question would be, how is she there
one second and gone the next?" Taglio asked
tensely.

"Press play."

The moment the tape started, the woman vanished.
In the blink of an eye. The fence was still there. The
trees were still there. But the woman was gone.

It was as if she'd stepped off the face of the earth.

Impossible.

But then, Lassiter knew better than anyone that
nothing was impossible.

"It must be the mist," Taglio said. "Somehow it created an optical illusion."

"Were any of the alarms tripped?"

He shook his head. "There's no way she could get through the lasers without all hell breaking loose." He glanced up at Lassiter. "You want me to put the camp on alert?"

"No, not yet." Lassiter was still watching the video, which now showed nothing more than mist swirling around the fence. "Let me have a look around first. I'll let you know if I find anything. In the meantime, don't mention that tape to anyone else."

Taglio shot him a look, but whatever was on his mind he kept to himself. "You're the boss. But just for the record, you never answered my question. How can a person just disappear like that?"

Lassiter shrugged. "I think you answered it yourself. It must have been some kind of optical illusion."

"Yeah, that must have been it." But Taglio didn't sound convinced, and his expression was anxious as his gaze moved past Lassiter to the open doorway and the gathering darkness beyond. "Or else…"

"Or else what?"

Taglio's gaze lifted and something that might have been fear flickered in his eyes, giving Lassiter a glimpse of vulnerability in the younger man that he suspected few people had ever witnessed. Taglio seemed almost embarrassed by what he had to say. "Maybe she isn't human."

Lassiter frowned. "What the hell are you talking about?"

"A ghost, Lassiter. I'm talking about a damned ghost."

LASSITER TRIED to laugh off Taglio's supernatural explanation, but he found himself shivering even though the night was warm and humid.

But Tag had it all wrong, Lassiter thought grimly as he climbed into his jeep and headed over to Sector Seven. The woman on the video wasn't the ghost. Lassiter was. He'd died a long time ago and he had some pretty damning proof that he should have stayed dead. Dead and buried in a watery tomb that now rested on the ocean floor hundreds of feet below the surface.

For a moment, the claustrophobic memories threatened to engulf him, and he could hear the cacophony of clanking metal and human screams slowly making their way to the surface. He shoved them away, buried them deep and kept driving.

He checked the fence along Sector Seven, but the metal hadn't been cut and the alarms were still set. The woman couldn't have gotten inside the camp. But just to be on the safe side, Lassiter drove the perimeter of the compound, making sure the guards were at their posts, and then he checked all the buildings.

The mess tent and rec hall were deserted, but he could see Kruger and Martin Grace still at work in the office, heads bent low, their expressions gloomy. They appeared to be arguing, but what compelling business kept them at it for so long, Lassiter had no idea. He didn't interrupt them this time. He had other things on his mind.

Parking the jeep, he crossed the interior of the compound on foot and checked the infirmary. The place was run by a man named Angus Bond, an Australian expatriate Kruger had dug up from somewhere who claimed to be a doctor. Bond had padlocked the door to keep the more potent drugs from falling into the wrong hands. Or so he said. But it had been Lassiter's suspicion for quite some time that old Angus wasn't above a little self-medicating. The padlock was probably more self-serving than precautionary.

Lassiter started to walk away when the sound of breaking glass stopped him short. He turned and put an ear to the door.

Someone was inside.

His first thought was that Angus had returned early from his day off, but Lassiter had seen the Aussie head off to Santa Elena just before lunch, and the good doctor never came back early or sober from a furlough.

Besides, how would Angus get through a door that was padlocked from the outside?

How would anyone get through that door?

A ghost, Lassiter. I'm talking about a damn ghost.

CURSING SOFTLY, Melanie whipped the scarf from her head and quickly wound it around the cut on her wrist.

Damn! She was getting blood everywhere.

And everything had been going so well until that point. She'd made it inside the compound without being detected. Located the infirmary and gotten inside without any problem. The locked medicine cabinet had presented the first real challenge, but she'd solved that by simply smashing out the glass front. No problem, except when she'd reached inside, she'd cut her wrist on a shard.

But even worse, the sound of shattering glass had been like a gunshot in the quiet. Someone might have heard the noise and would soon come to investigate. Melanie knew she had to hurry.

Fighting off a wave of dizziness from the sight of her own blood, she directed her penlight into the cabinet, playing the beam over the vials and bottles of medicine.

Whoa, some heavy-duty stuff there. OxyCotin, Percocet, Demerol. And some good old-fashioned morphine.

Tempting, but not why she'd come there.

Skipping the drugstore heroine, she went straight for the antibiotics, scanning the labels until she found what she needed. Quickly she stuffed the packets of tetracycline into the leather bag she wore draped over her shoulder.

A slight noise, nothing more than a swish of air, sent a chill up her spine, and slowly she turned toward the door.

A man stood just inside, almost hidden by shadows. Even so, Melanie could tell that he was tall, broad-shouldered, muscular. His features were indistinguishable, but she knew his gaze was on her. A cold, sharp, penetrating stare that cut her right to the bone.

He was dressed like a soldier. Camouflage jacket and pants. Rugged boots. A rifle barrel jutting over his shoulder, and he carried a handgun that was pointed at her.

She knew at once who he was, and her whole body went slack with fear.

El guerrero del demonio…

"¿HABLA USTED Inglés? Do you speak English?"

The woman didn't answer, just stood staring at him, unblinking, as if frozen. But Lassiter knew she understood him. Now that he'd gotten a better look at her, he could tell she was American by the way she carried herself, by the clothes she wore, the cut of her blond hair.

"How the hell did you get in here?" he demanded.

Still she didn't answer.

Slowly, she held up her hands as she began to back away from him.

"Stay where you are," he warned. "Don't move."

She continued to back toward the window, and Lassiter guessed her intent. "Stop!"

He rushed her, but she turned quickly, took a step toward the window and…disappeared.

Vanished into thin air.

Without thinking, Lassiter opened fire.

Chapter Two

"Let me see that wrist," Dr. Wilder commanded as he reached for Melanie's hand.

She put it behind her. "It's fine. Just a scratch."

His gaze turned reproachful. "Then why have you been hiding it from me all day?"

"I haven't. We've both been busy, that's all." Which was true. They'd had a steady stream of patients coming into the clinic for hours with ailments ranging from dementia to dysentery, and Melanie, who had come to the clinic four days ago to volunteer, had been kept so busy she'd barely had a moment to spend with Angel.

But the child's condition had been steadily improving. Her fever was down, the cough had subsided, and her breathing was finally normal. Both the oxygen and the IV had been removed, and with continued antibiotic therapy, Dr. Wilder was cautiously optimistic for a full recovery.

What would happen to the child once she was well enough to leave the clinic, Melanie didn't want to contemplate. She'd watched enough cable news back home to know the miserable plight of war orphans in countries like Cartéga.

"Melanie?"

She glanced up to find Dr. Wilder waiting patiently. "Your arm, please."

With a heavy sigh, she held out her hand, palm up, and Dr. Wilder carefully unwrapped the bandage she'd put around her wrist earlier that morning. The cotton was dotted with blood.

He looked up, his usually placid gray eyes now stern and ominous. "This is a very serious cut."

"It looks worse than it is." She tried to snatch her hand away, but Dr. Wilder held on firmly.

"It should have been sutured immediately. Why didn't you come to me?"

"I already told you, the less you know of my whereabouts last evening, the better off you'll be."

"This happened last night? At Kruger's compound?"

"No comment."

His features tightened. "How did it happen? Who did this to you?"

The angry, possessive note in his voice startled Melanie. They'd only known each other a few days, but they'd bonded through their mutual concern for Angel. Their friendship had developed rapidly during the crisis, which was unusual for Melanie. She didn't make friends easily or quickly, although her reckless behavior in high school *had* made her quite popular for a time, she thought dryly.

"No one did it to me. It was an accident. Let's just forget it."

"Easy to say until you develop a nasty infection," Dr. Wilder scolded. "Now hold still."

The door opened and Blanca, Dr. Wilder's nurse, stuck her head around the corner. Tossing back her long black hair, she eyed them curiously for a moment before she spoke. She was a young woman, Melanie's age perhaps, with delicate features and a curvaceous figure reminiscent of old Hollywood. The word *lush* always came to mind when Melanie saw her.

But Blanca's eyes were her most striking feature. Dark, wide and soulful, they glinted with suspicion every time she turned her gaze on Melanie.

The woman's instant and overt animosity was something Melanie still didn't understand.

"There is a man here to see you, Doctor," Blanca said in Spanish.

"English, please, Blanca." Dr. Wilder barely glanced up. "What does he want?"

He still held Melanie's hand, and Blanca's curiosity turned into a scowl of disapproval as she continued to observe them from across the room. "He said it was official business. A matter of extreme importance," she said in heavily accented English.

"He'll have to come back." Dr. Wilder released Melanie and began gathering supplies to suture her wrist.

"Wait a minute," Melanie said. "He could be

with the Ministry of Health. Maybe you should see him.''

Dr. Wilder gave a scornful laugh. ''The minister won't even return my phone calls. I highly doubt he'd send an emissary in person to meet with me.''

''What should I tell him?'' Blanca asked.

''Just what I said,'' Dr. Wilder replied curtly. ''I'm with a patient. He'll have to come back later. In an hour.''

Blanca's mouth tightened, but she left the room without a word and closed the door more soundly than necessary behind her.

''She seemed upset,'' Melanie said. ''Maybe you should go see who this man is.''

Dr. Wilder shrugged. ''Blanca is quite capable of taking care of the matter.''

''She does seem efficient,'' Melanie said carefully. ''How long has she worked for you?''

''A few months. Why?''

''Oh, I don't know. I just get the impression she's very protective of you.''

He turned away quickly, but not before Melanie saw a look of embarrassment flicker over his features. ''I'm going to give you a local, but it may still sting a bit.''

He was hiding something, she decided. Obviously, he didn't want to discuss his relationship with Blanca, but why? Was there something going on between them that Melanie had somehow missed?

If so, that would go a long way in explaining

Blanca's attitude, particularly if she regarded Melanie as a potential rival for Dr. Wilder's affection.

But if she only knew, Melanie thought with a grimace. Romance was the last thing she needed. And besides, what man in his right mind would ever understand, let alone accept, this…thing she could do?

Melanie didn't even understand it herself, but she knew instinctively that no good would come of it.

Where science is corrupted, evil often flourishes.

Dr. Wilder's warning suddenly came back to her, and her hand jerked reflexively.

He looked up. "I'm sorry. Am I hurting you?"

"Not much."

"I'll try to be quick."

He was as gentle as he could be, but thirteen stitches later, Melanie was fervently wishing for a hit of the Percocet she'd seen in the infirmary last night.

"I'M DR. WILDER. My nurse said you wanted to see me?"

"Jon Lassiter."

Neither man offered the other his hand. Instead, Dr. Wilder walked around his desk and motioned to a chair across from him.

"Thanks, but I prefer to stand," Lassiter said.

"As you wish." Dr. Wilder took a seat and folded his hands on the desk. "What can I do for you?" His voice was surprisingly calm, considering how tense he'd seemed when Lassiter had been ushered into his office.

"I work for Kruger Petroleum. We had an intruder in our compound last night."

Wilder lifted his brows. "I'm sorry to hear that, but what does it have to do with me?"

"The only thing missing were antibiotics. An odd choice, considering there were several opiates within easy reach, including morphine. Not a big demand on the black market for tetracycline."

Wilder grimaced. "You obviously aren't aware of the latest epidemic."

"I know about the fever," Lassiter said. "I also know that you have a patient here at the clinic, a girl about five years of age, who has typhuslike symptoms. Correct me if I'm wrong, Doctor, but the treatment for an infection caused by *rickettsia bacterium* is heavy antibiotic therapy, preferably tetracycline or chloramphenicol."

Something flickered in Wilder's eyes, but his expression never changed. "Are you accusing me of stealing your antibiotics, young man?"

"You don't match the description of the thief."

"Then I ask you again, what does any of this have to do with me?" Impatience had crept into Wilder's voice, but something else was there, too. Lassiter had the distinct impression Wilder was protecting someone.

"The thief was wounded in the robbery," he said. "I need to know if you treated anyone late last night or sometime this morning with a fairly deep cut, probably on one of her hands?"

"Her?"

"The intruder was a woman."

Dr. Wilder shook his head. "I've seen no one, male or female, with such an injury."

"What about a gunshot wound?"

Alarm flashed across his face. "A gunshot wound?"

"The intruder came under heavy fire," Lassiter explained. "She might have been wounded."

Wilder's mouth tightened. He suddenly looked very angry. "I've seen no gunshots wounds, either."

"You're sure about that?"

"Positive."

Lassiter knew the man was lying. The infinitesimal tick at the corner of his left eye gave him away. "I understand you have a young woman working at this clinic who does match the description of the intruder. Blond. About five foot seven."

"I'm afraid you're mistaken," Dr. Wilder said coolly.

Lassiter placed his hands on the desk and leaned forward. He could see something dark in the doctor's eyes. Fear? Contempt? A little of both? "Let me give you a warning, Doctor. I don't like playing games any more than I like being made a fool of in front of my employers."

Wilder said scornfully, "You would place a higher premium on your pride than on a child's life?"

Lassiter straightened. "Then you admit the drugs were brought to this clinic."

"I admit no such thing." Dr. Wilder pushed himself back from his desk and rose. "But if they had been, any rational man, any *moral* man, would see that the end justifies the means when an innocent child's life is at stake. Now if you'll excuse me, I'm very busy. I trust you can show yourself out.''

Lassiter strode across the room, then paused at the door to glance back. "If you did have such a woman in your employ, I'd ask that you give her two messages, the first being that in future, if she needs drugs, she might try asking for them. And second, there are some places in the world where a thief would be made an example of by having her hands chopped off in the public square.''

"If that's a threat…''

Lassiter smiled. "Just another friendly warning. So long, Doctor.''

He pulled the door closed between them and headed down the dim, narrow hallway toward the exit. Wilder's nurse, who was lurking in the corridor, jumped back to allow him room to pass. He suspected that only moments earlier, she'd had her ear pressed to the door, listening to every word being said in Wilder's office.

But as their gazes met briefly, she looked at Lassiter with neither guilt nor fear, but with a cool, deadly calculation that was more than a little disturbing.

FROM HER HIDING PLACE across the street, Melanie watched the man come out of the clinic and pause on the steps as his gaze went up and down the street. She shrank back into the alley, certain that *el guer-*

rero del demonio would have the ability to zero in on her even in the shadows, or in the middle of a crowd, or a hundred miles away.

They say he has…special powers.

Melanie shivered as she glanced around the corner of the building. He was minus the rifle and the camouflage gear she'd seen last night. Today he wore jeans and a snug black T-shirt that seemed at once nondescript and sexy. He might have been a good-looking tourist out for a bit of sightseeing—except for the rigid way he carried himself and that cold gleam she knew would be in his eyes.

Even from across the street, she could see the bulge of his biceps beneath his short sleeves, the depth of his chest through the cotton shirt. He was lean and muscular, a fighting man in the prime of his life. A mercenary who killed people for money, and Melanie had the impression he was very good at what he did.

Her stomach tightened as she watched him. He was looking for her, she knew that. He must have followed the trail of blood, so to speak. The clinic was the logical place to start his search.

How long before he gave up?

Or would he give up?

With one last glance down the street, he climbed into the jeep and made a U-turn in the street, heading north, toward the mountains. But Melanie knew he'd be back.

Her heart pounding uncomfortably, she waited until his vehicle was out of sight before she left her hiding place and headed in the opposite direction, toward downtown.

The population of Santa Elena was less than five thousand permanent residents whose meager livelihood depended on the tourists who came there to visit the cloud forest and the nearby Mayan ruins. The main thoroughfare ran through the heart of downtown, where a bustling open-air market catered to the foreigners and dilapidated buses dodged potholes, chickens and children playing soccer in the street.

Melanie's hotel was in the center of the village, a three-story terra-cotta building with wrought-iron balconies and potted hibiscus. A lush courtyard, hidden behind stone walls heavily draped with bougainvillea, provided a cool, shadowy oasis for guests needing a respite from the hot midday sun.

As she entered the Hotel del Paraíso, Melanie was struck again by the Old World charm of the lobby. A huge fountain, surrounded by tree ferns, bubbled in the middle of the stone floor while palm-leaf fans twirled lazily overhead.

She nodded to the clerk behind the desk as she made her way to the elevator and shoved home the wrought-iron gate. The elevator clanged its way to the third floor, where her room was located at the end of a long, dim corridor.

The room was large and airy, with a private bath and a view of the street that Melanie had requested. She was quite comfortable with the accommodations, but she knew if she planned to stay in Santa Elena for much longer, she'd have to find a cheaper place.

When her mother had died a few months ago, she'd left Melanie the bulk of her estate, but taxes had depleted a substantial portion of the inheritance. And Melanie's most recent job as a cocktail waitress hadn't allowed her to contribute much to the nest egg. Still, it would last her for a while if she was careful. Luckily, she was not a person given to consumer excesses. The basics were really all she needed—food to eat, a roof over her head, clothes on her back.

Stripping, she took a quick shower—a difficult task with one hand that had to be kept dry—then dressed in fresh jeans and a white cotton blouse she'd picked up at a thrift store in Houston before she'd caught a plane to Cartéga. Grabbing her bag, she left the hotel again, intent on finding a quiet place to have a drink and watch the sunset.

This time of day, the hotel terrace would be full of tourists, mostly Americans and Asians, who would have just gotten back from their trek to the cloud forest or the ruins. Their excited chatter could be entertaining at times, but today Melanie's nerves were on edge. She needed peace and quiet, a chance to think.

Heading down the street to a tiny café she'd discovered her first day in Santa Elena, she found a table on the patio, ordered a pineapple juice and then, settling in, let her mind wander.

"You must be new here."

The Australian accent startled Melanie so thoroughly she realized she must have drifted off to sleep. Alarmed by the lapse, her gaze shot to the man who stood over her table.

He was older, mid-fifties at least, with a haggard face and thin, white hair that brushed the shoulders of his lightweight suit.

Melanie knew she had never seen him before, yet there was something oddly familiar about him. "I beg your pardon?"

"I asked if you were new here. I come in often, and I don't believe I've seen you in here before." He put out a hand. "Bond. Angus Bond."

She couldn't help but smile at the way he introduced himself. She shook his hand. "Melanie Stark."

He held up a frosted glass garnished with a wedge of lime. "May I buy you a drink, Melanie?"

She nodded to her juice. "I already have one, thanks." She'd meant it as a polite brushoff, but something about him, that familiarity, made her say impulsively, "But you're welcome to join me if you like." What the heck? He looked harmless, save for a nasty scratch down the left side of his face, and there was something irresistible about a man with an Australian accent, no matter his age.

"I'd like that very much." He drew out a chair and sat down, then took a long, thirsty pull from his gin and tonic.

"Nectar of the gods," he said with a sigh.

"I thought that was wine."

''Not in my paradise.'' He grinned and took another swallow. ''So what brings you to Santa Elena, Melanie? The cloud forest or the ruins?''

''I intend to see both. How about you?''

He shrugged. ''I've lived off and on in Cartéga for quite some time now. Santa Elena has always been a favorite haunt of mine. I like the quaintness.''

Melanie lifted a brow in surprise. ''You live here? Judging by your accent, I would have guessed you'd just left Melbourne a few days ago.''

''Queensland, actually. I'm a banana bender, as they say.'' He grinned and saluted her with his drink. ''As for the accent, old habits die hard.''

''I know what you mean,'' Melanie murmured. She realized then why he looked so familiar to her. The evidence was there in his face. The excesses and the abuses. But it was his eyes that were the true giveaway. They were flat, emotionless, empty. She'd seen those same dead eyes years ago, in rehab. And in the mirror.

''So what do you do here?'' she asked him.

He toyed with his glass. ''Right now I'm working for an American oil company that has a drilling site about thirty miles north of town. Kruger Petroleum. Ever heard of it?''

Melanie almost choked on her drink. ''I don't think so.''

''They're a small, independent outfit, but they appear to be flush with cash. The owner, Hoyt Kruger, is a hands-on kind of guy. He supervises every aspect of the operation.''

"What kind of work do you do for him?" Melanie tried to ask casually.

"I run the infirmary. I'm a doctor."

It was all she could do not to spew juice from her nose. He ran the infirmary? Then he had to know about the break-in last night. Was that why he'd sought her out? Because he knew she was responsible? What was this? Some kind of fishing expedition? A trap?

"Santa Elena is a small place to have two doctors," she said carefully.

He glanced down at the bandage on her wrist. "I take it you've made the acquaintance of our illustrious Dr. Wilder. Nothing serious, I trust?"

"No. Just a careless accident."

"I sympathize." His smile was rueful as he ran a finger down the scratch on the side of his face. "What happened? If I'm not being too forward by asking."

Melanie hesitated. "I...broke a mirror in my hotel room. Luckily, I'm not the superstitious type."

"Then you obviously haven't been in Cartéga long enough."

"What do you mean?"

"It's a very superstitious country. The Cartégans love their legends. Haven't you heard about la Encantadora who lives in the cloud forest and uses the mist to lure men to their death? Or the ghosts of the Mayan priests who wander the ruins—" He broke off as his gaze went past Melanie's shoulder to the street. "Speak of the devil..."

Melanie turned to see what had drawn his attention. Her breath caught when she saw the man from the clinic climbing out of his jeep.

She whipped back around, trying not to show her distress. "Do you know that man?"

Bond's mouth tightened. "He works for Kruger. Euphemistically speaking, he's in charge of security, but…" His voice trailed off and he glanced away.

Melanie, sensing something in his tone, leaned toward him slightly. "But? What were you about to say?"

Bond looked suddenly uneasy. "Let me put it this way. He may be in charge of security for Kruger, but if I had a daughter, Jon Lassiter would be the last man on earth I'd want her to be alone with."

Melanie nervously glanced over her shoulder. Lassiter was making his way down the street toward the café. She didn't know whether he'd spotted them or not, but she wasn't about to wait around and find out.

She rose from the table. "I'm sorry, but I really have to go."

Bond gazed up at her in surprise. "So soon?"

"Yes. I…just remembered an appointment. It was a pleasure meeting you, though."

"Oh, believe me, the pleasure was all mine, Melanie."

When she reached into her bag for money, he held up his hand. "No, please. Allow me. I insist."

Melanie hesitated. "In that case, thank you very

much. Maybe I'll see you here again. The drinks will be on me next time.''

"I'll hold you to that.''

She could feel his gaze on her as she walked away, but it wasn't the leer of an older man admiring a younger woman. It was more innocent than that. For all his obvious vices and hard living, there was something guileless about Angus Bond. Something a bit sad.

But Melanie didn't have time to dwell long on the Australian, because as she left the patio and headed down the street, she turned and saw that Jon Lassiter had entered the café. He glanced up suddenly, and when he saw her, he said something to Angus, then started toward her.

Melanie spun around and headed in the opposite direction. Halfway down the street, she spied him again. He was even closer now, gaining on her steadily, although they were both trying not to draw attention.

Up ahead, a group of tourists had disembarked from a decrepit bus. Melanie hurried to infiltrate them, hoping to disappear among the chattering, excited vacationers.

Turning a corner with the crowd, she grabbed a peasant blouse from an outdoor rack in the market and hurried inside the dim shop.

"¿Me puedo probar esto, por favor?"

The ancient shopkeeper lazily waved a palmetto leaf fan in front of her face as she pointed to a dressing area in the back—a ragged blanket strung across one corner.

"*Gracias.*" Melanie dashed to the back and scurried behind the blanket. She fervently hoped that Lassiter would follow the tourists down the street, at least for a block or two. By the time he discovered she was no longer with them, he'd have no idea where she'd gone—

"*Perdón.*"

Melanie's legs trembled at the sound of his voice. She shrank back in the corner, hoping the shopkeeper wouldn't give her away.

"I'm looking for an American," he said in Spanish. "A young, blond woman. Very attractive. Have you seen her?"

"I saw the *Americanos* go by here," the shopkeeper replied. "They talk and laugh very loudly, but they don't spend their money in here." Her voice held a heavy note of regret. "Something for you perhaps?" she asked hopefully. "A gift for *su esposa? Su amiga?*"

"Nothing today," he said curtly. "*Gracias.*"

When their voices fell silent, Melanie assumed he'd left the shop, but she didn't want to press her luck. She remained behind the curtain for several minutes longer, then glancing around to make sure he'd gone, she carried the blouse to the shopkeeper and pulled some bills from her bag.

The old lady gave her a toothless smile of gratitude.

"Thank you for not giving me away," Melanie

said. She glanced around. "Could I ask another favor of you, *por favor?*"

"*Sí.*"

"Is there a back door I can use?"

"*Sí, por aquí.*" She got up and Melanie followed her to the back of the shop and down a grim little corridor that opened into a foul-smelling alley.

Stepping outside, Melanie glanced back at the woman who hovered in the doorway. *"Muchas gracias."*

The woman nodded, her black eyes gleaming with an emotion Melanie couldn't define. "That man, he is a bad one. A devil," she said in halting English, then, crossing herself, lapsed back into Spanish. *"Vaya con Dios."*

Melanie had no trouble making the translation. Go with God.

Chapter Three

A few minutes later, Melanie hurried into her room, bolted the door, then stood leaning against the frame as she closed her eyes and tried to catch her breath.

That had been close. Way too close.

But how long before Lassiter found her here?

And he would find her. In a place the size of Santa Elena, it would be easy to check all the hotels. Even if he didn't yet know her name, he had a description of her. He might even be knocking on her door within the hour.

Question was, would he come alone or would he bring the police?

In hindsight perhaps the better option would have been to face him back at the clinic or at the café where witnesses were present. After all, what had she done that was so terrible? She'd stolen drugs to save a young girl's life. Even if Jon Lassiter couldn't appreciate the distinction between that and petty thievery, surely the authorities would.

But what if Lassiter, or even Kruger himself,

wouldn't let it go? What if they pressured the police to arrest her? Make an example of her? Spending the next twenty years in a Cartégan jail wasn't Melanie's idea of growing old gracefully, but then, there were ways out of almost any prison, as she well knew.

She could have used those ways to get away from Lassiter earlier, but she hadn't wanted anyone on the street or the old lady in the shop to witness her vanishing act. Melanie had come to Santa Elena looking for answers, which meant she had to ask questions, and the last thing she needed was for the locals to become suspicious of her, let alone afraid of her.

She crossed the room and dragged her suitcase from the closet, but not to pack. Instead, she removed the stack of letters from inside, then lay down on the bed and propped herself against the headboard.

Plucking the top envelope from the packet, she stared at the handwriting. Her father's handwriting, she now knew. The letter had been sent from Cartéga six months ago.

She didn't open it because she didn't have to. She knew the contents by heart.

…I want to see Melanie on her birthday. Tell her I'll be waiting for her in the clouds…

Melanie didn't recall much about her father—what he'd looked like or even the sound of his voice—and yet the meaning of his words had come to her instantly. And with it, a memory of the last time they'd been together.

Melanie had been five years old, small for her age,

but adventurous even then. And impulsive. Already looking for that next thrill.

"Push me higher, Daddy!" They were in the backyard of their home on Long Island, testing out the new swing set she'd gotten for her birthday. "Higher!"

"You're going high enough, Melly Belly," her father had laughed. "If your mother could see you now, she'd have my head."

Funny how Melanie could remember the conversation so vividly and yet she still couldn't picture her father's face. Couldn't conjure up the sound of his voice no matter how hard she tried. Only his words came back to her.

"Higher!" she'd screamed. "I want to touch the clouds with my toes!"

"I know a place where you really can touch the clouds," he'd told her.

"Take me there!"

"Someday I will."

"Not someday. Tomorrow!"

"It's a long way from here, in a little country called Cartéga. I've been reading about it. You have to go way up into the mountains to touch the clouds. We can't go tomorrow, but we will soon. You and me and Mommy. We'll all touch the clouds together."

"Then push me higher," Melanie demanded, "so I can touch that cloud right now!"

Presently, her father stopped pushing her, and Melanie leaned back so far to look at him that she almost tumbled from the swing. "Why did you stop?" she pouted.

"Careful, you'll fall out," he warned.

"No, I won't."

"Hard head," he said affectionately. But there was a look in his eyes that made Melanie sad for some reason. "You think you're invincible, don't you."

"I don't know. I think I want you to push me some more."

"I can't. I have to go inside and…take care of some things."

"What kind of things?"

"Work kind of things." He knelt and placed his hands on her shoulders. "This trip we talked about. Let's keep it a secret for now, okay? Don't mention it to anyone."

"Not even Mommy?"

A shadow flickered across his features. "No, not even Mommy. We'll let it be a surprise. Right now, I have to go in and get some work done."

"I'll come with you."

"No. You stay outside and play. I won't get anything done with you around."

"But it's no fun out here without you," she protested.

"Sure it is. You just keep swinging. Pump your legs the way I taught you. That's it."

Melanie continued to swing after her father had gone inside, but her heart really wasn't in it. She didn't like being alone. She let the swing come to a stop, then lazily rocked herself back and forth with her toes.

After a bit, she began to have a strange feeling that she wasn't alone. She looked up, hoping her father had come back outside, but instead, she saw that a man had entered through the back gate.

Even though the day was warm, he wore a long, dark coat and a hat pulled low over his eyes. Melanie had the impression he'd been watching her for several minutes, and her heart started to pound in fear. She didn't like him watching her. He scared her. She wanted to get off the swing and run inside the house as fast as she could, but even if she could make her legs work, he blocked her path to the back door. So she sat on the swing, watching him watch her.

"Hello, Melanie," he finally said.

His voice made creepy crawlies go up her spine. She clutched the chains of the swing.

"You need to come with me now," he said, and Melanie shook her head. She wanted to scream for her father, but she couldn't make her throat work, either. It was like having a bad dream with a monster coming for you and you couldn't move.

The man walked slowly toward her. Her voice broke free then, and she screamed for her father. She screamed and screamed. "Daddy! Daddy!"

He didn't come out of the house, though, and as the man moved even closer to her, Melanie suddenly realized that someone else had come up behind her. The second man grabbed her, and before she had time to struggle, he pressed a cloth over her mouth and nose.

And that was Melanie's last memory until four years later.

She was sitting in that same swing, rocking herself to and fro and marveling at how easily she could touch the ground now. The back door opened, and Melanie looked up, hoping to see her father, but instead, her mother was the one who came out. At least, she thought it was her mother. She couldn't actually remember what her mother looked like, but this woman…*seemed* like her mother.

The woman carried a trash bag over to one of the metal garbage cans and tossed it inside. As she turned back toward the house, she must have caught a glimpse of Melanie out of the corner of her eye. She did a double take. Stared for a moment. And then her hand flew to her heart.

"Melanie? Oh, my God…oh, my God…" She started running toward Melanie, but her legs gave out and she sank to her knees. She was screaming, crying, holding out her arms.

Melanie hesitated for just a split second, then she got off the swing and raced across the yard. Her mother grabbed her and squeezed her until she could hardly breathe.

"Oh, my baby," her mother kept whispering over and over. "My baby, my baby!"

After a few moments, she held Melanie away from her so that she could look at her. She reached up to touch Melanie's face, her hair. "You're so tall! But it is you, isn't it? Of course, it's you.'' Her gaze darkened as she glanced past Melanie. ''But...how did you get here? Where have you been?''

Melanie didn't know where she'd been or how she'd gotten back home. She didn't know anything except that she wasn't supposed to ask questions.

When she didn't answer, her mother pulled her back into her arms and held on tightly. ''It's okay, baby. It doesn't matter how you got here. Don't even think about it. You're home now and that's all that matters.''

She led Melanie into the house, leaving her side only long enough to make a phone call and, a little while later, to answer the doorbell. A strange man came into the kitchen where Melanie sat eating a sandwich.

''Do you remember Dr. Collier, honey?'' her mother asked anxiously. ''He's going to have a look at you, make sure you're okay.''

The last thing Melanie wanted was to have a stranger poking and prodding her. But Dr. Collier was gentle and he didn't do anything to upset her. Not too much, at least.

After he was finished, he motioned for Melanie's mother to follow him out into the hallway. Melanie got up from the table and tiptoed across the room to listen at the door.

''Physically, she seems fine, but we need to take her to the hospital where she can have a thorough examination.''

''But you said she's fine,'' her mother protested.

"I said she seems to be fine. Janet, that child has been missing for four years. God only knows what she's been through."

"I've been thinking about that," her mother said softly. "Whoever had her has obviously taken good care of her. Her clothes are clean, and she looks healthy. I think someone saw her that day, a couple who couldn't have a child of their own, perhaps, and they decided to take her. She was such a beautiful little girl, and always so beguiling. Remember how she was? Maybe their guilt finally got the better of them and they decided to bring her back to me."

"If that's the case, why can't she remember them? Why can't she answer even the simplest questions about her abductors?"

But it was as if her mother hadn't heard him. "I'm sure they loved her very much."

Dr. Collier didn't say anything for a long moment, then in a low voice, "You have to call the police, you know."

"The police—"

"Melanie was abducted. They'll have to question her, find out what she knows about her kidnapper."

"I don't want to talk to the police." Her mother started to cry again. "She's come back to me. That's all I care about."

But the police did come later that day, and they talked to Melanie for a very long time. She couldn't answer any of their questions. She couldn't describe the men in the backyard that day. She didn't know where they'd taken her, or what, if anything, they'd done to her. She didn't know where she'd been for the past four years or how she'd finally gotten back home. She didn't remember anything, not even her own face.

All she knew was that she wasn't supposed to ask questions. Questions were forbidden.

It was late by the time the police finally left. Melanie's mother led her back to her room and tucked her in bed. She sat on the edge, fussing with the covers as if she had to get them just right or Melanie wouldn't be able to sleep.

"Mommy?"

Her mother put a hand to her mouth, as if overcome with emotion. Tears streamed down her face.

Melanie said contritely, "I'm sorry."

"Oh, baby, you have nothing to be sorry about."

"I'm sorry I made you cry."

"These are happy tears. When you called me Mommy…it's just been so long…I thought…" Her mother dried her eyes with the back of her hand. "It doesn't matter what I thought. We're together now, and that's all that counts."

She gathered Melanie into her arms and hugged her as if she would never let her go. When she finally did pull away, Melanie said softly, "Mommy, where's Daddy?"

"Your daddy had to go away, honey."

"Why?"

She bit her lip. "Because it made him too sad to stay here after you were gone."

"Is he dead?" Melanie asked worriedly.

"No, he's not dead. He just went somewhere far away from here."

"Where?"

"Houston, I think. Do you know where that is?"

"Texas?"

"Yes, that's right." Her mother looked surprised that Melanie knew the answer.

"Why didn't you go with him?" Melanie asked.

Her mother hesitated. "Because someone had to be here when you came back."

Melanie thought about that. "Can he come home now?"

Her mother looked as if she was about to cry again. Melanie was suddenly sorry she'd asked about her father. "No, honey, he can't come home. He's…I don't even know if he's still in Houston. But wherever he is, I'm sure he's fine." She leaned down and kissed Melanie's cheek. "Everything's going to be okay, Melanie, I promise. I'll take such good care of you from now on. When you wake up in the morning, I'll fix you blueberry pancakes. That was always your favorite breakfast. Maybe later we'll go to the zoo. Just the two of us." Her voice broke as she smoothed her hand down Melanie's hair. "Sleep now, my precious little girl, and when you wake up, it'll be as if you never left."

And her mother had tried very hard to make it so even when the police detective in charge of the case had implored her to seek professional help for Melanie. His advice had fallen on deaf ears.

"She's not talking to a shrink," her mother insisted. "I won't put her through that."

"Mrs. Stark, Melanie has been through a very traumatic experience. She's blocked all memory of the time she was missing."

"You seem to think that's a bad thing," her mother said. "I happen to think it's a blessing. I'm glad she can't remember what happened to her. I hope she never does."

"But what if those memories come back to her someday? She won't be prepared to cope—"

"I appreciate your concern, but I know what's best for my daughter."

And that had been the end of it. The last time Melanie had talked to the police about her abduction. She and her mother never spoke of it again, either. Her mother seemed convinced that if they pretended hard enough, those four years would just go away.

And for a while, that missing time did seem like nothing more than a bad dream. They sold the house on Long Island and moved to a little town in upstate New York. Melanie started back to school as if she'd never been absent a day, let alone four years. Wherever she'd been, she'd obviously been schooled. If anything, she was far ahead of her peers. She made new friends, played on a softball team, did all the things that normal nine-year-old girls do. On some level, she might even have been happy.

But at night, when she lay alone in her room or when she dreamed, that's when the screams would come back to haunt her.

Melanie soon learned that putting her hands over her ears wouldn't block the torment. Nothing would. But that didn't stop her from trying. As she grew older, she experimented with new and increasingly destructive means to shut out the screams. There was a time during her teenage years when she'd been completely out of control.

But her mother still wouldn't seek counselling for Melanie. She insisted that all Melanie needed was unconditional love, which she gave to her daughter in abundance. Through the truancy and all the wild parties and even rehab, her mother never judged, never scolded, never punished. If anything, she seemed to love Melanie even more.

Finally, after high school, things started to improve. In spite of her self-destructive behavior, Melanie had always excelled in her studies, and when she was accepted into a premed program at a local university, it seemed as if she'd finally gotten her life back on track. She even fell in love.

She and Andrew were inseparable all through college, but then, just weeks before graduation, he'd come to her and told her their relationship wasn't working for him.

Melanie had been devastated. "Why?"

He gazed at her sadly. "Because what I see when I look into your eyes scares the hell out of me, Mel."

Wounded, Melanie bit back her tears. "What *do* you see?"

He gave a helpless shrug. "Nothing. All I see in your eyes is emptiness."

He'd walked out of her life that day, and just two weeks before getting her degree, Melanie had dropped out of school. For the next few years, she drifted from place to place, from job to job, from relationship to relationship.

And then six months ago, when her mother had died unexpectedly, Melanie had returned home to try to put their affairs in order. She'd come across the stack of letters while cleaning out her mother's closet. They'd been stored in an old shoe box shoved to the farthest corner of the top shelf.

The first one had been sent from Houston more than twenty years ago. Melanie hadn't recognized the handwriting on the envelope, and she'd hesitated to read through her mother's personal correspondence. But then curiosity had gotten the better of her, and she'd opened the letters one by one, stunned to learn that they were all from her father. All these years, when Melanie hadn't heard a word from him, he and her mother had kept in touch.

The early letters, written while she'd still been missing, had been outpourings of grief and guilt. Then later, after Melanie had returned, his letters took on a disturbing paranoia.

I'm sure the police are pressuring you to allow her to see a psychiatrist, but you have to remain strong. If Melanie remembers what happened to her, they'll take her away again. And this time, they won't let her come back.

She mustn't remember, Janet. Melanie must never, ever remember....

As she'd read through those strange letters, Melanie had been bombarded with questions. Who were "they"? And why was her father's fear so great that he wouldn't even come to see her?

Nine years after Melanie's return, the letters had stopped, leaving a ten-year gap in the correspondence. The final one had been posted from San Cristóbal, Cartéga just weeks before her mother's death, but something seemed to be missing in the exchange, leaving Melanie to wonder if perhaps her parents had had some other form of communication in the years between the letters.

Her father now seemed to be pleading for a chance to see Melanie.

I know you don't agree, Janet, you've made your position perfectly clear. But I think it's time Melanie and I meet. She's had such an unhappy, troubled life. I think I can help her.

Our daughter will be twenty-eight in August. A grown woman. Old enough, surely, to make her own decision about this.

If you decide to let her come—and I pray that you will—I should probably have you warn her that she won't recognize me. Neither would you. I had my appearance altered a long time ago, but even more than the surgery, the years away from you and Melanie have taken a toll.

I can't tell you what it would mean to me to

see her again, to have one last chance to tell her how much I love her, how much I've always loved her. And how very sorry I am for my part in what happened to her. My guilt is a hell I live with every day of my life. Please give me this one last chance for redemption.

I want to see her, Janet. I want to see Melanie on her birthday. Tell her I'll be waiting for her in the clouds.

Melanie rose from the bed and put the letters back in the suitcase. Shutting and locking the lid, she shoved the case back into the closet, then walked over to the window to stare out at the twilight.

It was stuffy inside the room. She opened the door for a moment, letting in a fragrant breeze, but she didn't step out on the balcony. She was careful to remain in the shadows as she gazed down at the street.

Gooseflesh prickled along her arms, although the evening was mild. Perhaps it was the tears drying on her face that made her cold. Or the loneliness that suddenly engulfed her.

I can't tell you what it would mean to me to see her again, to have one last chance to tell her how much I love her, how much I've always loved her. And how very sorry I am for my part in what happened to her.

His part in what had happened to her. *His part.*

What had he meant by that? Did his guilt stem from a father's inability to protect his daughter?

From the fact that if he'd stayed outside with her as she'd begged, she wouldn't have been taken?

Or was his remorse the result of something far more sinister?

Had he been a party to her abduction? Did he know who had taken her and why? Had he known for those four years where she was and what was happening to her?

Did he know what they'd done to her?

Melanie had no idea of the answer to any of those questions, but she knew she had to find her father and confront him. She had to ask him point-blank why he felt so guilty. She had to make him look her in the eye when he told her the truth.

Then she would know.

And all those years of running and hiding and trying to block out the screams would finally be over.

Chapter Four

She wasn't a natural blonde.

That little detail was oddly telling to Lassiter, because it was yet one more piece of evidence that Melanie Stark had secrets. Dark ones. And her real hair color was the least of them.

He stood at the foot of the bed gazing down at her. Light streaming in through the balcony window glimmered off the gold streaks in her hair and made her skin look soft and pale.

And he could see a great deal of skin. She'd kicked off the covers in her sleep, and she lay on the sheet in nothing but a light-blue tank top and white silk panties.

Even in her sleep, she looked like trouble.

There was an air of recklessness about her. A hint of hedonism.

Lassiter had nothing against hedonism, particularly in a woman who looked like Melanie Stark. Not that she was especially beautiful. Her features were too imperfect—even apart from the telltale dark roots—

for that. Eyes that were a little too widely set, a nose that was slightly off center.

But her lips, easily her best feature, were lush and tempting, and her body…

He drew a sharp breath as his gaze moved over her. The body, he had to admit, came pretty damn close to perfection. Either she had great genes or she'd been giving her gym membership one hell of a workout. She looked entirely capable of handling herself both in bed and out. Not exactly the type of girl you took home to Mother, but Lassiter's plans for Melanie Stark didn't include a trip back home to Mississippi, anyway.

She stirred in her sleep and sighed. Something inside him quickened and he knew that, for better or worse—and his instincts told him the latter—his life was about to take a drastic turn.

Who are you? he silently wondered as he stared down at her. *And where the hell did you come from?*

MELANIE CAME AWAKE with the terrifying certainty that she wasn't alone. Someone was in her room. It was every woman's nightmare to open her eyes and find a strange man standing over her bed.

But there were strange men and there were strange men.

At least Melanie recognized her midnight intruder, although she couldn't honestly say the knowledge gave her much comfort. Far from it. Especially considering the way he was staring down at her.

She gasped and scrambled up against the headboard. Clutching the covers to her chin, she said hoarsely, "Who are you? What do you want?"

"I think you know who I am, Melanie."

A cold chill shot through her. "How do you know my name?"

"I know a great deal about you. You'd be surprised."

The sound of his voice frightened her more than anything else. The timbre was at once smooth as velvet and jagged as broken glass.

He moved slightly, and moonlight fell across his face, giving her a glimpse of mesmerizing features. She couldn't seem to tear her gaze from his, and she thought fleetingly, *No wonder the old woman called you a devil.*

He was handsome, dangerous, darkly seductive. *El guerrero del demonio* in all his glory.

Melanie's gaze lit on the phone beside the bed and she lunged for it. But he was quicker. His hand clamped around her wrist and squeezed until she let go of the receiver, then he pushed her back against the headboard.

"Do you really want to call the police, Melanie?"

That voice. Those eyes. Dear God.

He was the kind of man she'd always been drawn to. Dark, dangerous, sexy as hell. But tonight, seduction was the last thing on Melanie's mind. All she wanted was to see him leave.

"If you get the police involved, I'll be forced to tell them you're the thief who's been stealing drugs from Kruger's infirmary," he said.

A tiny flame of anger melted through her fear. "I took the antibiotics to save a child's life."

"I don't give a damn about your motive."

"The police—"

"The police won't care, either. Your best chance is to make a deal with me, right here and right now."

Melanie shivered beneath the covers. If that was her best chance, she was in big trouble. "What do you want?"

He let the silence gather around them until Melanie could hear nothing but the pounding of her heart in her ears. She wanted to scream, but she hadn't been able to scream for a very long time.

"I want to know how you did it," he finally said.

Her grasp tightened on the blanket. "Did what? I don't know what you're talking about."

"Don't play stupid; Melanie. How did you do it? You were in the room with me one moment and gone the next. It was like you walked through an invisible doorway. I want to know how you did it."

She forced an icy edge to her voice. "Why should I tell you anything? You break into my room, threaten me—"

His smile in the darkness sent a tremor up her spine. "Do you know what they do to drug dealers in Cartéga?"

"I'm not a drug dealer."

"Try telling that to the police. This isn't back home, Melanie. In Cartéga you're guilty until proven innocent, and you were caught red-handed, so to speak." His gaze shot to the bandage around her wrist. "We've even got samples of your DNA, though God knows what they'd do with it down here. Chances are they'd throw you in the slammer without asking too many questions." He paused, taking a step or two back from the bed, but his gaze never lost hers. "Have you ever seen the inside of a Cartégan prison? After a year in one of those cells, your own mother wouldn't recognize you, and after twenty years…" He shrugged. "But then, after what I saw you do last night, the thought of a jail cell probably doesn't frighten you all that much, does it."

She tossed back her hair, trying for a bravado she was far from feeling. "If that's true, then your threat doesn't hold much water."

"Right. Except—" his gaze narrowed "—if you disappear from prison, or even from this room, I'll make sure you become the most wanted fugitive in this part of the world. Every *federal* in Central America will be looking for you. And that would make searching for your father damned near impossible, wouldn't it?"

She gasped. "How do you know about my father? *What* do you know about him?" When he didn't answer, she lashed out in anger. "You've been in my room before, haven't you. You read my letters. Who let you in here, you bastard? Who did you have to bribe?"

"First things first." His voice seemed to deepen with menace. "I've got a proposition for you."

Her heart hammered against her ribs. "Not even in your wildest dreams, assho—"

"Not that kind of proposition." Even though she was thoroughly hidden by the sheet, his gaze moved over her in a way that made her shiver with dread. She hadn't been covered when she'd first awakened, though, and there was no telling how long he'd been standing there watching her sleep. He might even have touched her…

Melanie almost ripped a hole in the worn cotton where her nails clutched it. "If you so much as come near me…"

"Don't flatter yourself. You're not my type." He moved to the foot of the bed, as if to make his point. "Don't you even want to hear my deal? You should, seeing as how you have no choice but to accept it."

"There's always a choice, Lassiter."

"So you do know my name." He gave her a look she couldn't quite define in the darkness. "Tell me how you did it, and I'll tell you what I know about your father. I'll even help you find him."

She gazed at him in defiance. "I don't need your help. Besides, I wouldn't trust you with my own life, let alone my father's."

"You can. Trust me, that is. I don't mean you any harm. I just need to know how you did it."

"Why?"

He hesitated. "It's not every day someone disappears before your very eyes." He'd said it with irony, but there was a hint of something else in his voice, something that might have been desperation.

"It wasn't what it seemed," Melanie said, showing her own desperation. "It was just a trick. A smoke-and-mirrors kind of thing."

His voice hardened. "Then show me. Do it now."

She gave a helpless shrug. "I can't just do it at will. It takes time to set up. The lighting has to be just right—"

"You're lying."

She let exasperation creep into her voice. "Do you really believe someone can just disappear like that? Come on."

He was beside her in a flash, bending over the bed to grab her shoulders. His fingers dug into her flesh. "I saw you do it. I saw it with my own two eyes, and I'm not a man prone to wild imaginings. So, yes, I believe it. And if you don't tell me how you did it…"

"You'll what?" She gave him an insolent glare while her heart threatened to thrash its way out of her chest. "You'll call the police? Kill me? Go ahead. I'm calling your bluff."

She winced as his grasp on her arms tightened. His eyes burned into hers. "You don't want to do that, Melanie. You really don't. Not for your sake and especially not for your father's."

"If you hurt him, so help me—"

"Nothing will happen to your father. Not if you tell me what I want to know."

The desperation in his voice must have been her imagination, Melanie thought fleetingly, because now she heard nothing but danger. He'd killed before. Easily, from the looks of him. If she pushed him too far, she might give *him* no choice.

"Look at it this way," he said. "I saw what I saw. You're not going to bluff your way out of it, so what do you have to lose by telling me how you did it?"

He was right about that. He *had* seen her. The damage had already been done. And regardless of how hard Melanie tried to convince him that his eyes had deceived him, Jon Lassiter was nobody's fool. He wouldn't leave here until she gave him what he'd come for, and maybe not even then. But at this point, she really didn't have much to lose.

"Even if I told you the truth, you wouldn't believe me. There's no way I can make you understand it. I...don't even understand it myself."

"Try me."

She wavered, trying to think of a way to buy herself some time. "Let me get dressed first. I don't like feeling at such a disadvantage."

He straightened and stepped back from the bed. "Be my guest."

She bit her lip as she stared up at him. "At least have the decency to turn around."

"And give you a chance to do your 'smoke-and-mirrors thing'? I don't think so."

"I already told you. I can't do it at will. It takes time. Just give me a moment's privacy to get dressed. I promise I won't disappear."

He leaned toward her again, planting a hand on either side of her. Melanie caught her breath at his nearness, at the coldness in his eyes. "If you do disappear, let's get one thing straight. There's no place you can go that I won't find you. *No place*. You understand?''

She nodded, not daring to speak.

LASSITER WALKED to the foot of the bed and turned his back on her. What she didn't know, of course, was that he'd positioned himself so he could watch her in the dresser mirror. He didn't trust her even for a moment. No way was she going to play him for a fool. Again.

It was dark in the room, but enough light straggled in through the window that he could see her reflection as she rose from the bed. She turned to the side, and a glimmer of light outlined her full breasts as she drew the tank top over her head and reached for her shirt. As she fastened her buttons and then pulled on a pair of jeans, something flared to life inside Lassiter. It had been a long time since he'd watched a woman dress.

Walking across the room, she sat down in a chair near the windows and reached for the lamp.

"Leave it off," he ordered.

She let her hand fall to her lap. "I meant what I said earlier. Even if I tell you the truth, you won't believe me."

He sat down on the bed, still warm from her body, and regarded her across the room. "I've always had an open mind. So let's hear it."

"First you have to give me your word you won't do anything to harm my father."

"You tell me the truth, and I'll not only help you find him, I'll also do everything in my power to keep you both safe."

Her brows lifted in suspicion. "What makes you think we need your protection?"

"When a man runs out on his family, changes his appearance, hides out in a place like Cartéga, it's usually because someone is looking for him. Don't tell me that hasn't occurred to you. Don't tell me you haven't considered the possibility that someone may have followed you down here."

He saw her stiffen—in fear, he thought—before she shrugged in apparent defiance. "How do I know you're not the one who's looking for him?"

"Because if I were, he'd already be dead."

Her body shivered violently. "If you think that inspires my trust…"

"It should inspire fear," he said. "I don't know what you're involved in, but after what I saw last night, I'd say the stakes are pretty damn high. If you want someone watching your back, you'd better tell me the truth."

"And why in the world should that someone watching my back be you?" she demanded.

"Because who else is there, Melanie?"

That seemed to stop her, and she fell silent for a long moment as if she couldn't decide what to do. Then she drew a deep breath and released it. "All right. You've made your point. But the truth is I don't know how I do it. I'm being honest," she said quickly when he tried to protest. "I *don't* know. The

first time it happened was by accident. I found myself...let's just say, I found myself in a difficult position, and I literally willed myself through a wall. It
scared the hell out of me when I came out on the
other side. I didn't tell anyone about what I'd done
because I didn't want the men in white coats to come
and take me away. Back then, I was skating pretty
close to the edge as it was, so I tried to convince
myself I'd had some sort of weird dream or hallu-
cination. But when I was able to go back through the
wall...when I was able to do it over and over
again—''

"Wait a minute," Lassiter cut in with a frown.
"You told me earlier you couldn't do it at will."

She shrugged. "I can't just snap my fingers and
go *poof.* It takes intense concentration, a sort of re-
alignment of my consciousness, as well as the vibration of my body. You said it seemed as if I'd walked
through an invisible doorway and just disappeared.
That's a pretty accurate description. Except the doorways aren't made of wood or metal or glass. The
openings are a subtle shift in energy, light and vibration. But once you know they're there, your body
can pass through them just as easily as you can open
the door to my room and walk out into the hallway.''

Lassiter wished he'd let her turn on the light earlier, because he suddenly wanted to see the nuances
of her expression. "So what are you saying? When
you pass through one of these invisible doorways,
you're what? Entering another dimension?''

She gave an odd little laugh. "Sounds rubber-room worthy when you put it like that, but it's hardly a new concept. Certain principles in quantum physics suggest that the universe is made up of a framework of dimensions connected by these doorways. We're unaware of their existence because our physical senses only allow us to perceive our own three-dimensional reality. But what if our perception of reality is just an illusory phenomenon?''

"Meaning?'' he asked skeptically.

"Meaning that experiments on the subatomic level have determined that our own consciousness can and does affect matter outside our physical bodies. Therefore, consciousness can and does affect our perception of reality. That's the essence of the Quantum Theory of Observer-Created Reality. There is no such thing as an objective reality. It's all in our heads. Everything is consciousness. Remember that. You'll need to grasp that concept in order to understand the rest of what I have to tell you. That is…if you want me to continue.'' She gave him a doubtful glance, but it seemed to Lassiter that she was no longer reticent about talking to him. In some ways, she appeared almost eager, as if she found it a relief to finally have someone willing to suspend disbelief long enough to hear her out.

"Why didn't you use one of these invisible doorways earlier when you were running away from me?''

"I didn't want anyone to see me do it. And besides—'' she made a helpless gesture with her hand "—it's not something I like to do. It's not…normal.

And it's dangerous on the other side. Unstable some-how. I'm afraid once I've gone through, once I've 'phased,' the doorways will close up and I won't be able to find my way out. I'll just become energy or matter or…something.''

"How is it you can see these doorways when no one else can?"

She glanced away for a moment, and Lassiter had the feeling that she'd come to the part of her story that made her the most uncomfortable. "I can see the doorways because my mind has been programmed to see them. My consciousness has been altered to ac-cept them as part of my reality."

He frowned. "Are you talking about brainwash-ing?"

"It goes farther than that."

"Who programmed you?"

She got up and walked over to the window to stare out. "I don't know for sure. I've done some re-search…" Her voice trailed off as she moved rest-lessly back to her chair and sat down. "I think it goes back to my childhood. My family used to live on Long Island, not far from the old Montauk Air Force Station. When I was five, I was abducted from our backyard by two men whose faces and voices I can't recall. In fact, I have no memory at all until four years later when I was returned to the same backyard."

"Wait a minute," he said sharply. "This isn't some alien-abduction fantasy, is it?"

Melanie laughed again, this time with a hint of real

amusement. "I'm pretty sure the men who kidnapped me were human. But as far as what they did to me..." The laughter died away and she fell silent.

Lassiter went cold inside as he watched her. Her head was bent. She was staring at her hands, but he had no idea what she was really seeing. "Were the kidnappers apprehended?"

She shook her head. "I couldn't give the police anything to go on because I didn't remember anything."

"Did you ever try regression hypnosis?"

"My mother wouldn't allow it. She wouldn't allow any kind of therapy. We never even talked about what happened. She thought we were both better off not knowing. She managed to convince herself that some kindly couple had kidnapped me and had taken very good care of me until their guilt made them bring me back home."

"My God."

Her eyes closed briefly. "I know."

Those two words, spoken in such a soft voice, said it all. The despair and helplessness. The subtle edge of anger. No wonder once she'd allowed a tiny crack in the dam, it had all come pouring out. "So how did you cope with all this?"

"I didn't. Not very well, at least. I went through some pretty rough years. I guess for a while I tried to pretend right along with my mother that everything was fine, and maybe I could have convinced myself that it was if it hadn't been for the screams."

Her gaze lifted to Lassiter's. "The screams of the other children."

He went almost deathly still. "There were other kidnapped children where you were?"

"I can't remember them, but I have a sense that there were…a lot of them."

Her restlessness suddenly infected Lassiter, and he got up to pace. "You have no idea who abducted you or why? Or where you were taken?"

"I didn't for years. But after the first incident of phasing, I began to do some research. The natural place to start seemed to be my abduction. I was stunned to find literally mountains of information about the Montauk Air Force Station and a covert, subterranean operation known as Project Phoenix. Have you ever heard of it?"

Something clicked in Lassiter's mind, but he shook his head. "I don't think so."

"What about the Philadelphia Experiment?"

He stopped his pacing and stared at her. "That's one of those stories that conspiracy nuts get off on. Like who shot JFK. They're always backed up with a lot of rumor and speculation but very few facts."

"But like all legends, there's usually a grain of truth in them," Melanie said. "And as this story goes, a U.S. Navy ship undergoing an experiment using magnetic fields back in World War II disappeared from Philadelphia Harbor. I don't mean it went missing. It literally dematerialized. When the *Eldridge* returned to its original position hours later, the sailors aboard were all violently ill. Some of them were insane. Some were dead. And at least one crew member was missing. The survivors were eventually dismissed from the military as unfit to serve.''

''So you're saying when the ship disappeared, it entered this other dimension?''

''That seems to be the consensus, yes.''

Lassiter rubbed the back of his neck. ''Wasn't there a movie made about this experiment? Are you sure you're not just regurgitating the Hollywood version of what happened?''

''All the information I gathered was out there long before any movie was ever made,'' Melanie said. ''And I'm not trying to sell this to you as fact. I don't know if any part of it's true. I'm simply telling you the trail I followed when I tried to figure out what had been done to me. The technology is grounded in quantum physics and seems to lead back to the experiment that was conducted on that ship back in 1943.''

Lassiter started to pace again. ''Go on.''

''After the ship rematerialized, the scientist in charge of the operation, Dr. Nicholas Kessler, was so appalled by the condition of the crew that he tried to sabotage his own project in order to ensure that the experiment could never be repeated. The congressional oversight committee was terrified that the technology would fall into the wrong hands, so they cut off funding and shut down the project entirely. But you can't un-open Pandora's box. A clandestine rogue agency got involved. Their private funding allowed them to operate beneath the radar of congressional oversight, as well as the CIA and NSA, and they persuaded Dr. Kessler's protégé, a man named Joseph Von Meter, to continue the experiments.''

"At Montauk."

She nodded. "Yes. In a series of underground bunkers. At first, Dr. Von Meter concerned himself with the side effects suffered by the ship's crew. He concluded that the intensity of the magnetic fields in the original experiment had produced a kind of artificial reality around the ship. An abnormal plane of existence that had no relation to our three-dimensional reality. Therefore, anyone trapped within the magnetic field became severely disoriented, sometimes to the point of insanity."

"In other words, their physical bodies were placed in a situation their minds couldn't accept."

Melanie nodded. "That's exactly right. Von Meter experimented with ways to overcome this problem by creating reference points for the individual test subjects. I don't really understand how it worked, but it had something to do with generating a false electromagnetic background that would give their physical bodies something to lock on to. A false earth link, in effect. Later, when Project Phoenix expanded into altered states of consciousness and observer-created realities, a much simpler and effective method was devised. The test subjects were simply given a new reality."

"Who were these test subjects?" Lassiter asked.

"Initially, they used indigents and military personnel who had no families, but then they discovered that children were far more susceptible to altered states of consciousness than adults. Most of the subjects were males between the ages of nine and twelve. They were called the Montauk Boys, and their acceptance of engineered realities was so complete that they could phase in and out of dimensions without the use of computers or electromagnetic equipment.''

''How were they persuaded to accept these...what did you call them? Engineered realities?''

Lassiter thought he saw her shudder before she answered. ''A number of methods were used, including sleep deprivation. But fear was the prime motivator. Some of those children were literally scared out of their minds.''

It had suddenly become unbearably stuffy in the room. Lassiter walked over to the window and opened it. He stood for a moment, gazing down at the street as he tried to block the screams inside his own head.

''Shall I go on?'' she asked softly.

He nodded without looking at her.

''When they grew older, the Montauk Boys were also trained in combat, but I'm not sure if they were physically trained or simply programmed. They became a kind of special-ops team of super soldiers known as Delta Force, although oddly enough, there seems to be no connection to the army's elite commandoes. But even as far back as Vietnam, there were rumors inside the military of a special-forces team connected to Project Phoenix that could enter a heavily guarded building behind enemy lines, carry out a mission and return to their home base without ever having been seen.''

Finally Lassiter turned to her. ''You said most of the test subjects were boys. Why did they take you?''

''My father was a scientist who worked for the government.'' She hesitated. ''Or at least, that's what I was always told. Now I believe he was part of the Montauk projects.''

He gazed at her in disbelief. ''You think your own father had you abducted and subjected to mind-control experiments?''

Lassiter couldn't see her expression clearly, but for a moment, he could have sworn he saw tears glistening in her eyes. Then she glanced away. ''That's what I'm here to find out. And now that I've told you everything, I need to know what you plan to do with the information I just gave you.''

He turned back to the street. ''We had a deal, remember? You tell me the truth and I'll help you find your father.''

''I don't need your help,'' she bit out. ''I need you to stay out of this. I need you to go back to guarding Kruger's oil wells and forget what you saw last night. Forget what I told you just now.''

''I don't think I can do that.''

''Why not? Look, everything I just told you, I got from the Internet, mostly from so-called conspiracy-theory Web sites. For God's sake, any normal person would have already written me off as some sort of mental case.''

"Not if they'd seen what I did last night," Lassiter said. "You may not want to admit it, but you're involved in something that has the potential to turn the world as we know it upside down. And that's a very dangerous situation to be in."

"I can take care of myself."

Whether she really believed that or not, Lassiter had no idea. She didn't strike him as the naive type, but he had no doubt she could be stubborn.

"Besides," she said with a frown, "why should you get involved? Why do you care about any of this?"

"I care. Let's just leave it at that." He turned and started walking toward the door.

"Where are you going?" she asked anxiously.

"It's late, and I have to be up early in the morning. And I've got some thinking to do."

"About what?" When he didn't respond, she said in desperation, "Why can't you just leave me alone?"

He still didn't answer her.

"Lassiter!"

He stopped and glanced over his shoulder.

She rose from her chair and started toward him, as if she meant to somehow physically restrain him. "I need to know something else before you go."

"What?"

Her hand trembled as she pushed back her hair. "How did you get in here? The safety latch is still on the door, so you couldn't have used a key. Did you climb up the lower balconies and jimmy the lock on the French door?''

He gave a slight shrug. ''That would be one way to do it.''

Then he turned, took a step toward the door, and…disappeared.

Vanished into thin air.

Melanie sank to the floor, not knowing whether to laugh or cry.

Chapter Five

By midafternoon the sun had burned away the low-lying fog that drifted down from the mountains, but in the higher elevations, where guerrilla activity was heaviest, a lingering mist—and what it might hide—had Lassiter worried.

He'd been dogged by a premonition of doom all day, and the feeling had only grown stronger when Danny Taglio called him on the radio that afternoon and asked to meet him in Sector Seven.

Lassiter had a pretty good idea what was on the younger man's mind. Taglio had clearly been disturbed by what the surveillance camera had picked up two nights ago, and he wasn't the kind of man to let the matter drop.

He paced anxiously near the fence when Lassiter arrived at the rendezvous point a few minutes later.

Lassiter parked the jeep and got out. "What's going on?"

Taglio shrugged, but there was something in his eyes, a telltale gleam of nerves that made him glance away. "Hell if I know, Lassiter. I keep coming over here trying to figure out how she did it."

Lassiter frowned. "What's to figure out? I thought we agreed it was just an illusion created by the fog."

"I'm not so sure about that now."

Lassiter let the barest hint of derision creep into his voice. "What's the matter, kid? Still think you saw a ghost?"

Taglio's expression turned defensive. "Hey, you have to admit, the way she disappeared was weird as hell."

Lassiter shrugged without comment.

"But even if it was an optical illusion," Taglio persisted, "that still wouldn't explain what she was doing out here in the first place. Santa Elena is the nearest village, and the only other civilization within miles is the guerrilla encampments in the mountains. What the hell was she doing out here all alone in the jungle?"

"Maybe she got lost." Lassiter kept his expression neutral, but his tone dropped a couple of octaves, sending the clear and unmistakable message that he didn't appreciate having his time wasted like this.

But Taglio ignored the warning. "I've been giving this some thought, and the way I figure it, she was either nosing around trying to get a fix on our security or she came out here to meet someone. And I'm thinking maybe it was both."

"Meet someone? Like who?"

Taglio paused, his gaze shifting away from Lassiter's. "Why don't you tell me? You disappeared awfully fast that night. And you refused to put the camp on alert. I guess I'm wondering why.''

''You got something to say, spit it out,'' Lassiter said coldly.

Taglio's gaze slid back to his. ''All right, I will. You wouldn't be playing both ends against the middle, would you, Lassiter?''

The accusation caught Lassiter by surprise, mostly because it was so far off the mark. ''What the hell are you talking about?''

Taglio pulled a videotape from his jacket pocket and held it up. ''I'm talking about the fact that one of the cameras picked up an intruder and you not only refused to put the camp on alert, you didn't even report it to Kruger.''

''Not that I need to justify myself to you, but why would I bother Kruger with something like that? You said yourself none of the alarms were tripped.''

''Maybe because somebody had already disarmed them. And maybe that somebody was you.''

Taglio had guts. Lassiter had to give him that. ''You better be careful here, Tag. You understand me?''

''Oh, I understand all right.'' The younger man suddenly seemed emboldened. ''I've got a few sources of my own around here, and they've been telling me for weeks that an outsider, maybe someone connected with this camp, is working with the rebels. I think that someone is you, Lassiter. I think you sold Kruger out.''

''You're full of it, Taglio.'' Lassiter turned back

to the jeep, but the other man caught his arm. Lassiter flung off his hand and gave him a look that had made men with far more experience that Danny Taglio squirm.

He took a step back, still clutching the tape. "Give me one good reason why I shouldn't turn this over to Kruger."

Lassiter gave a low, humorless laugh. "You think you got something on me, go ahead. Show it to Kruger. And after you do, pack up your gear and get the hell out." He started walking toward the jeep.

"Maybe the tape alone doesn't prove anything," Taglio said behind him. "But I think Kruger would find it pretty damn curious that you didn't want anyone else to see it. And I think he'd be even more interested to learn you were in that woman's hotel room last night."

That stopped Lassiter cold. His features went tight with anger as he spun back around.

Taglio's eyes glinted in satisfaction. "I thought that would get your attention. See, as it happens, I was in Santa Elena myself last night. I spotted you hanging around outside Hotel del Paraíso, so I decided to go in and have a little talk with the desk clerk. I gave him your description, slipped him some bills, and he couldn't have been more helpful. He said you'd been in earlier asking questions about an American woman named Melanie Stark."

"And that proves what exactly?" Lassiter said in a deadly calm voice.

Taglio shrugged. "That's what I wanted you to

explain last night, but I couldn't find you after I left the hotel. Seems Melanie Stark isn't the only one who knows how to disappear," he said slyly. "So I went off to have a few drinks, and then later, I swung back by the hotel before calling it a night. I knew the woman's room number because the clerk had given it to me earlier. I decided to go up and have a look-see for myself, but she wasn't alone. I heard voices coming from her room, and one of them was yours."

Lassiter paused a heartbeat, then said very softly, "You were on duty last night, Taglio. Deserting your post is a serious offense."

"We both left the army a long time ago. Military rules don't apply to us."

Lassiter smiled. "That's right, they don't."

He took a step toward the younger man, and alarm flashed across Taglio's face. Then he glanced up at the surveillance camera and gave a shaky laugh. "Better not do anything impulsive, Lassiter. We're being watched."

"So we are. For now."

"Look, you may not believe this," Taglio said, "but I didn't get you out here to threaten you. I'm trying to warn you."

"About what?"

The younger man paused. "I'm not the only one who knows where you were last night. Somebody else followed you to the hotel. Somebody else is interested in that girl."

Lassiter grabbed the front of the man's shirt and hauled him up hard. "What are you talking about?"

"Hey, take it easy." Taglio gave him a shaky smile. "Look, I know you didn't sell Kruger out on general principle. Somebody must have made you an offer you couldn't refuse. All I'm asking for is a piece of the action. Cut me in and I'll give you a name."

Lassiter jerked him forward. "Give me a name, and I might give you a head start to the border."

"You won't kill me, Lassiter."

"No? You sure about that?"

Taglio swallowed, not looking at all sure. "You want to know who's interested in the girl, don't you?"

Lassiter shoved him away in disgust.

And a split second later, Taglio hit the ground.

It happened so fast, Lassiter thought at first the younger man had stumbled. But then the sound of gunfire registered, and he saw blood leaking from a hole in Taglio's forehead. Lassiter's auto pilot kicked in then, and he dived for cover behind the jeep, dragging Taglio with him.

Quickly, he checked for a pulse and heartbeat, and when he detected neither, he got out his radio to put the camp on alert. Then, adjusting his frequency, he roused Angus Bond in the infirmary.

"Sniper fire in Sector Seven," he said. "I've got a man down."

The Aussie's voice sputtered over the static. "What's his condition?"

"He's dead, but there could be other casualties."

"I'm standing by."

Lassiter couldn't tell if Bond was sober or not, but from Taglio's point of view, it didn't much matter.

He glanced down at the wound. It was a clean shot. Couldn't have been more dead center if Taglio had had a bull's-eye painted on his forehead. The sniper was either very lucky or very good. Or both.

Returning his radio to his belt, Lassiter reached up and grabbed a pair of binoculars from the front seat of the jeep and then carefully positioned himself between the tire and bumper to scour the mountainside.

He tried to trace an invisible line from where Taglio had been dropped to a point anywhere from five hundred to fifteen hundred yards up the mountainside. But even the lower elevations were covered with dense rain-forest vegetation and, combined with the heavy blanket of mist, rendered the sniper invisible.

Lassiter took off his cap and placed it over the barrel of his rifle, then exposed it over the hood of the jeep.

The shot was instantaneous, dead center through the front of the cap.

Question answered. The sniper was good. But he'd also given away his position, and that was all Lassiter needed.

There was a doorway, a portal not ten feet away. He could see a very faint glimmer of light. His bloodstream tingled with the change in energy, and he could feel the vibration of his body subtly alter as he lunged toward the opening.

He experienced the familiar tug of resistance as he went through, then an immediate rush of energy, a blur of light, and in the blink of an eye, he emerged on the mountainside to the rear of the shooter.

Immediately, he took cover and then inched his way toward the sniper's blind, mindful of his surroundings.

But he was too late. In the almost infinitesimal time it had taken him to travel through the wormhole up the mountain, the sniper had vanished.

A chill shot up Lassiter's spine as he walked over and picked up the weapon the killer had left behind.

The rifle was a surprise. He expected a rebel sniper to have gotten his hands on a Soviet-made Dragunov by way of Cuba, but this weapon was an M21, a semiautomatic sniper rifle that had been used by the U.S. military years ago. It was obsolete now, but the M21 had once been the primary sniper rifle of the Vietnam War.

Something Melanie had said last night suddenly came back to Lassiter.

…even as far back as Vietnam, there were rumors inside the military of a special-forces team connected to Project Phoenix that could enter a heavily guarded building behind enemy lines, carry out a mission, and return to their home base without ever having been seen.

Lassiter gazed around the deserted mountainside as the blood in his veins turned to ice.

"BUT YOU CAN'T release her yet," Melanie protested in alarm. "She's still too weak, and besides, she has nowhere to go."

Dr. Wilder sighed heavily. "I'm not talking about releasing her today. Angel is still a very sick child and she isn't out of the woods yet. But you have to understand something, Melanie. We have only a few beds here at the clinic, and we have to reserve them for the patients who need them the most. If Angel's recovery continues as I expect it to, the time will come in the very near future when we'll have to make other arrangements for her."

Melanie bit her lip. "You mean an orphanage, don't you."

"I don't see that we have any other choice. If we can't locate family or friends who are willing to take her in…" He trailed off on a shrug. "What else can we do?"

He was right, of course. If Angel's family couldn't be located, then the little girl would eventually have to be placed in an orphanage; the alternative was begging in the streets. The choices were heartbreakingly few and very often brutal for children like Angel. That was reality in Cartéga, and neither Melanie nor Dr. Wilder could change it no matter how much they might wish to.

Even if Melanie had the means to take the child in herself, the Cartégan government was very strict about foreign adoptions. A single American female wouldn't stand much of a chance. The best she could hope for was to somehow find the child's parents or persuade another family to take her in.

"Why don't you go back to your hotel and try to get some rest?" Dr. Wilder gave her a sympathetic smile. "Carmen told me you came in before six this morning. You must be exhausted."

"I'm all right," Melanie murmured, but in truth, she could feel the weariness settling into every muscle and bone in her body.

After Lassiter had left her room the night before, sleep had been impossible. Melanie had alternated between tossing and turning and staring out the window.

Finally at daybreak, she'd given up on rest and had come down to the clinic to see if she could help with the patients. The only nurse on duty at that hour had been Carmen Santiago, a pleasant, middle-aged woman who'd been delighted to have an extra pair of willing hands.

But as busy as Melanie had been all day, she still hadn't been able to keep her thoughts from wandering to Jon Lassiter. It wasn't every day you saw someone disappear before your very eyes, she thought dryly, using his own words. Witnessing his phasing had stunned her—she'd never actually seen anyone do it—but afterward, she couldn't honestly say that she'd been shocked or even surprised that he could. On some level she must have already known.

Why else would he have pursued her so relentlessly? Most people would have looked for a logical explanation for what he'd witnessed at the infirmary two nights ago. And barring any reasonable conclusion, they would have decided it was their imagination or a trick of the light.

But Lassiter had never doubted his eyes even for a moment because he *knew* it was possible. That explained why he'd gone to so much trouble to hunt her down.

But it didn't explain why he'd been so adamant that she tell him how she did it. Didn't *he* know?

Or had he, like her, discovered the ability quite by accident?

Melanie's first experience had occurred at the rehab facility. Only twenty-four hours clean and sober and she'd been climbing the walls, certain she'd go out of her mind if she didn't find a way out of what she considered a prison.

When she saw the glimmer of light in the wall, felt the tingle of energy flowing through her bloodstream, she assumed she was having some sort of episode. And when she was able to pass her hands through the wall, she knew she'd finally gone off the deep end.

But something, desperation or instinct, made her walk through the wall. When she suddenly found herself outside the rehab center, she was terrified, certain that she really had lost her mind. But then she did it again—could do it over and over—and she finally had to accept the reality of her ability.

Strangely enough, when provided the opportunity, she hadn't run away from rehab. She'd gone back into her room, climbed into bed and pretended that nothing had happened. But the knowledge that she could leave whenever she chose gave her the courage to stick it out. She'd finished the program, and for nearly a decade, had taken nothing stronger than an aspirin.

But there wasn't a day that went by she didn't think about her addiction. There wasn't a morning she didn't wake up wondering how she'd get through the rest of the day.

"Melanie?"

She mentally clicked back to Dr. Wilder. "Sorry. I must have drifted off."

"You look dead on your feet." He came around the desk and put an arm around her shoulders. "Come on. I'll walk you out."

He gently but firmly led her down the hallway to the front door. "I'll see you in the morning, but don't come in too early. You need to get some sleep. After all, aren't you supposed to be on vacation? Volunteering at a clinic isn't much of a holiday."

"It has its rewards," Melanie said with a smile. She gave him a wave as she walked away.

But she'd gone only a block or so when she realized she'd left her bag back at the clinic. Her room key was inside, but more important, her father's letters.

Since Lassiter's sudden appearance last night, Melanie had had every intention of transferring the letters, along with her passport and spare cash, to a rented safe in the hotel, but she hadn't yet had a chance.

Now she wavered, trying to convince herself that the bag would be perfectly safe in the clinic until morning. The desk clerk at the hotel could let her into her room. There really was no need to go back.

But she knew herself too well. She wouldn't be able to get any rest until her father's letters were put somewhere safe. Those letters were her only link to him—and to her past—and she didn't want to lose them.

Turning, she hurried back to the clinic and let herself in the front door. The desk and hallway were deserted, and she assumed Blanca and Dr. Wilder were with patients. But as she headed down the corridor to the tiny closet where the staff stored their personal belongings, she heard raised voices coming from Dr. Wilder's office.

Normally, Melanie wouldn't have given the sound much thought. And she certainly wouldn't have eavesdropped on a private conversation if she hadn't heard her name spoken with such heated animosity. As it was, she hesitated just outside the door, unabashedly listening in.

"…understand your problem with her, Blanca. I really don't. She came here to volunteer her services when she could just as easily be spending her time reclining by the pool at her hotel and sipping coconut rum punch with the other *turistas*. I would think you'd be grateful for her help."

Blanca muttered something too low for Melanie to

understand, then she said more loudly and in perfect English, "She is going to bring us nothing but trouble, and you know it."

"I know no such thing."

"She brought *him* here, didn't she?"

"And I got rid of him," Dr. Wilder said impatiently.

"But for how long? He'll be back. Others may come, too. As long as she's here, we'll be constantly looking over our shoulders."

"You're exaggerating. Working yourself up into a state when there's really no need. I have everything under control."

"But I don't understand," Blanca said in a wounded tone. "Why do you want her here so badly?"

"It's like I said. We can always use an extra pair of hands."

"And that is the only reason?"

"*Mi gorrión pequeño,* what else could it be?"

Melanie had already guessed their relationship was more than just professional, at least on Blanca's end. But to hear the distinguished Dr. Wilder call a woman half his age "my little sparrow" was a bit unsettling, although there was no reason it should be. Blanca was young, but she wasn't a child.

And this conversation was really none of Melanie's business. Even though she was burning with curiosity, she knew the only decent thing to do was leave quietly and pretend she'd heard nothing.

She might have done exactly that if Blanca hadn't

said in a low, menacing tone, "If she means nothing to you, then why let her stay here? Let me get rid of her."

"I have my reasons for keeping Melanie close. Let's just leave it at that."

"But—"

A door slammed somewhere nearby, and Melanie jumped. Inside the office, Dr. Wilder and Blanca fell silent. Then Blanca hissed, *"¿Qué fue eso?"*

"Someone slammed a door. Nothing to be alarmed about, but I'll go check it out."

Melanie glanced around frantically for a place to hide. There were doors all up and down the corridor, but none near enough to give her cover before Dr. Wilder made it across his office and glanced out.

Without thinking, she moved across the hallway, closed her eyes, put out her hands and passed through the wall.

She emerged into the room on the other side. Dr. Wilder's muffled voice sounded through the plaster. "It's okay. It must have been one of the staff leaving through the back door. Diego, perhaps…"

His voice faded, and only then did Melanie realize how hard her heart was pounding.

A soft gasp brought her around with a start, and she saw then that she was in a patient's room.

Angel watched her from across the room, her eyes wide and dark with terror. As Melanie started toward her, the little girl opened her mouth to scream.

Chapter Six

The official investigation into Danny Taglio's death was a mere formality and was concluded only hours after the shooting. An officer from the Santa Elena police force drove out to the compound, asked a few questions, wrote up a report and then left, thus washing his hands of the whole affair.

Since Taglio had signed on under Lassiter's command, the responsibility for the final arrangements fell to him. And since Lassiter had no idea where Taglio was from originally or how to get in touch with his next of kin—or even if Danny Taglio was the man's real name, for that matter—he'd made arrangements with a local mortuary for the body's removal and interment the following day.

There would be no funeral. No memorial service. No weeping widow or grief-stricken mother. Taglio would be laid to rest in foreign soil without benefit of song, prayer or eulogy.

The same fate awaited Lassiter someday. Which was fitting, he supposed, considering that his own interment should have occurred five years ago, at the bottom of the North Atlantic.

Instead, he'd awakened in a hospital with tubes and machines attached to his body and the echo of screams inside his head.

Weeks later, in spite of a full recovery, he'd been dismissed from the military as mentally unfit to serve. A fate worse than death for a man who'd never wanted anything more than to fight for his country. And now he was a man without a country.

"Lassiter?"

He roused himself from his reverie and stared across the desk at Angus Bond. The older man held up a bottle of gin he'd pulled from a desk drawer.

"Care to join me?" he asked, filling a glass. "I hate to drink with the flies."

"No, thanks."

"Still on duty, I suppose." Bond gave him a rueful salute with the glass before tossing back the contents.

"Have you had a chance to examine the body?" Lassiter asked.

Bond grimaced. "I had a look. But what you asked me to do…" He broke off as he poured himself another shot of gin. "I'm not a damned pathologist, Lassiter. I treat head colds, intestinal problems, stitch up the occasional laceration. Cutting open a man's skull, even with the proper instruments, is a gruesome business at best." He killed the second drink, then wiped the back of his hand across his mouth. "The poor boy's head is a mess."

"He doesn't have to look pretty," Lassiter reminded him. "There won't be an open casket."

"No, I suppose not," Bond muttered. But it was obvious he'd been affected by the idea of doing an autopsy.

"What can you tell me about the wound?" Lassiter asked.

Bond shrugged. "The bullet followed a fairly straightforward path through the brain. There was surprisingly little yawing or fragmenting. I've seen wounds like that in combat. A soldier takes a clean hit in the shoulder or leg, or even the chest cavity, then gets patched up and is sent back to his outfit in a matter of weeks or even days. In other words, Lassiter, if Taglio had been hit almost anywhere else besides in the head, he'd likely still be alive. Does that tell you anything?"

It told Lassiter quite a lot, in fact. The lack of fragmentation told him that the bullet was a full metal jacket, probably U.S. manufactured rather than German or Swiss. And the choice of nondeforming ammunition not only told him that the gunman's intent was to kill not maim, it also spoke of the killer's supreme confidence in his own abilities. Unlike most of the rebel snipers Lassiter had encountered, this man didn't need to rely on fragmentation. He was that good.

One shot. One kill.

"You said you'd seen this kind of wound in combat," Lassiter said. "Where?"

"In Vietnam." When Lassiter's brows shot up,

Bond gave a wry laugh. "You look surprised. Is it because you don't see me as the type to serve my country, or because you didn't know we Aussies had a presence in Vietnam? Most Americans don't, you know."

It was a little of both, Lassiter supposed. "Is that where you met Kruger?"

Now Bond looked surprised. "Why would you think that?"

Lassiter shrugged. "For some reason, I had the impression that you two go way back. I thought you might have served together in Vietnam."

Bond shook his head. "You must be thinking about his partner."

Lassiter glanced up. "Martin Grace? How do you know he and Kruger were together in Vietnam?"

"I don't know that they were together. But I do know Martin Grace was in Vietnam."

"How?"

Bond looked suddenly uneasy. "I probably shouldn't say anything, but..." He leaned forward and lowered his voice. "A few days after he arrived, Grace had a bad case of dysentery. When I gave him an injection of antibiotics, I noticed he had an unusual tattoo on his left arm. When I mentioned it, he flew off the handle and told me to mind my own business if I knew what was good for me. Then he bailed out of the infirmary like the devil himself was after him. The man's a bit of an arse, if you ask me."

Lassiter's own assessment of Martin Grace was

pretty much the same. "What did the tattoo look like?"

Bond refilled his glass. "Some kind of bird, I think. Actually, I'd seen it before on a patient I treated in Vietnam. That's why it caught my attention. This guy had been shot up by the VC and was in bad shape when they brought him in. He kept mumbling something about being with a special-forces team on some top-secret mission. Evidently, his unit was ambushed and he got separated from his mates. He kept rambling on about not being able to find a doorway. I thought he was delirious at first, but when I started asking him questions, he clammed up. Wouldn't even give me his name, rank and serial number. I got the impression he was worried he'd already said too much."

Bond finished his drink and poured yet another. "If the poor bloke hadn't died that night, he might have had to kill me," he said without humor.

AFTER THE FIRST few moments of shock, Angel hadn't appeared frightened at all by what she'd seen. In fact, she'd been excited and kept whispering in reverence, *"Usted es un angel."*

"No, sweetie, I'm not an angel," Melanie had assured her softly. She'd finally managed to coax the child back to sleep, and then she'd crept down the hallway, retrieved her bag from the closet and slipped out the back way.

All the way back to the hotel, she kept replaying the conversation she'd overheard between Dr. Wilder and Blanca. For the life of her, Melanie couldn't figure out why Blanca felt so threatened by her. Was it mere jealousy or something more sinister?

Was it possible she and Dr. Wilder could be involved in something illegal? Melanie wondered suddenly. It would make sense, then, that Blanca was so worried about Melanie's presence. Besides, if Blanca's concern stemmed from nothing more than jealousy, why had she pretended to speak only broken English when in fact she was quite fluent?

Something strange was going on at that clinic, but Melanie had no idea what it was. Or what it had to do with her.

I have my reasons for keeping Melanie close. Let's just leave it at that.

Her footsteps faltered as something else occurred to her. Was it possible that Dr. Wilder was the man she'd come to Santa Elena to find? Was it possible he was her father?

She quickly dismissed the idea. If he was her father, she would have known somehow. She would have felt something for him. There would have been some kind of clue, no matter how small.

But what she'd felt for Dr. Wilder was nothing more than respect for his abilities as a doctor. The bond that had developed between them was because of their mutual concern for Angel.

Although Melanie had to admit their friendship had developed rather quickly. And it was obvious that Blanca sensed something between them.

But her father?

Why wouldn't he have said something? After all, it had been his idea for her to come to Santa Elena.

Melanie started walking again. Her birthday was coming up in a couple of days at which time her father, according to his letter, would make arrangements to meet her in the cloud forest. Until then, all she could do was wait.

Hurrying into the hotel, she went straight up to her room. As she unlocked the door and stepped inside, the back of her neck prickled in warning. The subtle tingle of electricity and the barely discernible vibration sent a shiver up her spine.

She saw only a brief shimmer of light before the doorway closed, concealing the identity of the person who had been in her room a split second before she'd entered.

LASSITER CAME instantly awake.

His sleeping quarters consisted of a cramped cubicle tacked onto the end of the barracks with only a small window to let in light. But it was enough illumination to allow him to make out the dark silhouette hovering over his bed.

He acted on instinct. Bolting upright, he grabbed for the throat, then flung the intruder down on the bunk, squeezing his windpipe as he simultaneously ground a knee into the man's abdomen.

But the interloper wasn't a man, he realized almost at once. The fullness of her breasts beneath the skintight black top she wore gave her away, as did the long blond hair spilling from the black knit cap she'd pulled on.

Recognizing her, Lassiter eased the pressure on her windpipe and removed his knee from her stomach, but he didn't free her entirely. He kept her pinned between his knees in order to search for weapons. He hadn't trusted anyone in years, and he wasn't about to start now.

"Just take it easy," he said, "and nobody gets hurt."

The way he'd trapped her seemed to infuriate her. She clutched her bruised throat as she rasped, "You nearly killed me, you bastard."

"Best not to sneak up on a man while he's sleeping," Lassiter advised unrepentantly. He ran his hands down her body. The black pants and top fit her like a second skin. He could feel every curve, every muscle, every tempting inch of her body. She'd have to be pretty damn creative to hide a weapon in that outfit, but Melanie Stark had struck Lassiter from the first as a woman not without imagination.

She tried to jerk away from him. "What the hell do you think you're doing?"

"Searching you for weapons."

"If I had a gun you'd already have a bullet hole in your head," she said, deadly earnest.

He lifted a brow at her bravado. "Somehow you seem more like the switchblade type to me."

"Be very grateful I don't have a knife."

"Big talk from someone in your position," he goaded. But he had to give her credit. Most women who found themselves in her situation would have been begging for their lives by that time. Or on occasion, begging for something else. But not Melanie. She wasn't the begging type. She'd take what she wanted and then demand more.

And the speculation of just what those demands might entail fueled Lassiter's X-rated imagination. He let his hands linger in places where they had no business.

She said between clenched teeth, "Get your hands off me, you bastard."

"That's the second time you've called me a bastard in the space of a minute. You really need to work on your vocabulary. It's getting a little repetitious."

Her eyes flashed in the darkness. "How about this, then? Get your hands off me, you jerk. You asshole. You stupid…"

She tried to slap him, but Lassiter easily caught her hand. Grabbing her other wrist, he raised both arms over her head and leaned in closer.

He could barely make out her expression in the dark, but he knew that her eyes were gleaming with fury. She was breathing hard in her anger. For a moment, he remained transfixed by the rise and fall of her breasts.

Then something changed in her. The anger turned to something else, something…

He pressed his body against hers, letting her feel his arousal, and she went completely still, her gaze locked onto his.

He heard the small catch in her breath as her lips parted slightly, inviting him to kiss her.

When he didn't, she looked momentarily confused, and then her rage returned in full force. "You *bastard*," she hissed.

"So we're back to that, are we?" He slid off the bunk and reached for his pants. He could feel her gaze on him in the darkness, but when he turned, she quickly glanced away.

"Why did you come out here?" he asked gruffly.

"Not for that," she lashed out. "I want to know just what kind of scam you're trying to pull on me."

"I don't know what you're talking about."

Her eyes blazed in the darkness. "I'm talking about last night. I'm talking about how you left my room. Why didn't you tell me you could do it?"

"Because I wanted to find out what you knew first."

"Liar. You're one of them." She shot to her feet. "You've been sent here to keep me from finding my father."

"That's not true, Melanie. I want to find your father as badly as you do. I need those answers just as much as you do."

She gritted her teeth. "I don't believe you. You want something else or you wouldn't have come back and searched my room today."

"I haven't been anywhere near your room all day."

"Stop lying! It couldn't have been anyone else."

"And I'm telling you it wasn't me." He caught

her by the arms. "So why don't you tell me what this is all about so we can get to the bottom of it?"

She looked as if she wanted to wrest herself from his grasp, but her pride wouldn't allow her to engage in a struggle she was destined to lose. So she stood her ground and gazed at him with icy contempt. "When I let myself into my room this afternoon, I caught a glimpse of a doorway before it closed up. Who else could have done that but you?"

His grip tightened on her arms. "Did you see anyone go through?"

She lifted her chin. "No. But it had to be you."

"It wasn't me, Melanie," he said grimly.

She looked taken aback by the finality of his denial. "Then who…"

He lowered his voice. "Look, I agree we need to talk about this, but not here. Someone could hear us. Give me five minutes to get dressed and I'll meet you back at your hotel."

Her brows lifted. "Five minutes? It'll take a lot longer than that to drive back to Santa Elena."

"You drove out here?"

"How else would I get here?"

"I assumed…" He hesitated, shaking his head. "Never mind. Where did you leave your vehicle?"

"Just off the road, about a mile south of the main entrance."

He nodded. "I'll find it. Wait for me there."

When she started to turn away, Lassiter caught her arm. She looked up expectantly.

"Be careful getting out of here. Don't let anyone see you."

"No one will see me."

"Don't be too sure about that. We have surveillance cameras mounted all around the perimeter of the camp. One of my men saw you on the monitor and caught your little 'smoke and mirrors' trick on tape." At her alarmed expression he said, "Don't worry. He won't say anything."

"How can you be so sure?" she asked.

"Because he's dead."

MELANIE SHIVERED as she sat in her four-wheel drive and waited for Lassiter. She didn't mind admitting that it was nerve-racking being in the jungle all alone. There was a moon, but the huge strangler tree near where she'd parked blocked most of the light. She could only imagine the predators that prowled the forest at night, and the eerie sounds coming from the darkness fed her wildest fears.

When she saw Lassiter emerge from the trees a few yards in front of her vehicle, she breathed a deep sigh of relief. Then she immediately tensed. The moment of attraction between them earlier had unnerved her more than the jungle.

At least he was dressed now, but her mind immediately flashed to the way he'd looked leaning over her. The bulge of muscles in his forearms. The washboard ripple of his abdomen. Those eyes, that mouth…

Jon Lassiter was the hottest man Melanie had encountered in quite some time, and he was also the most dangerous. Just her type, unfortunately.

Men like him had never brought her anything but trouble. They were good for one thing only as far as she was concerned.

They sure as hell weren't the type you could count on. Not the type you could plan a future with, either. Melanie couldn't, in a million years, picture Jon Lassiter happily married and settled in suburbia.

But to be fair, she couldn't picture herself in a blissful state of matrimony, either. She had nothing against a casual affair, but the problem was, there was nothing casual about Jon Lassiter. She knew his type all too well. The relationship would be intense while it lasted. A passionate, consuming obsession. He would take her heart, twist it in every direction imaginable and then, when it was over, he would leave her, desperate and devastated, without a backward glance.

She stared at him nervously as he climbed into the vehicle beside her. "You still want to drive in to Santa Elena?"

He nodded. "I don't know about you, but I could use a drink."

"How will you get back?"

He gave her another strange look. "I'll manage."

Melanie reached to turn on the ignition, then paused. "Can I ask you something?"

He shrugged.

"You said the man who saw me the other night is dead. You didn't—"

"A sniper took him out earlier today," he said before she could finish.

"I'm sorry," Melanie said softly. "Was he a friend of yours?"

"I don't have any friends. And don't be sorry. Death comes with the territory. We all know the risks."

Melanie paused, her attention arrested for a moment by the grim resolve in his voice. "Didn't anyone notice the break-in at the infirmary?"

"Angus Bond came in drunk that night. He passed out cold, and when he woke up the next morning, he assumed he'd broken the glass out of the medicine cabinet when he fell into it. And he had a nasty cut on his face to prove it."

"He didn't miss the antibiotics?"

"No, but it would have been a different story if you'd taken the morphine," Lassiter said dryly. "So relax, okay? All the bases are covered."

His words seemed to confirm Melanie's first impression of Angus Bond. He was an addict and had been for years.

"Anything else you want to know?"

She reached for the ignition. "There's plenty I want to know. But I'll save it until after you've had your drink."

THE ROAD TO Santa Elena was pitted with potholes and deep ruts left from the last rainy season. As they bounced along, Melanie was forced to give her undivided attention to her driving. Neither she nor Lassiter said another word until she pulled into Santa Elena thirty minutes later, and then he gave her directions to an out-of-the-way bar.

The place was in a part of town Melanie had never seen before. The unpaved streets were narrow and dark and crowded with dilapidated bars and cantinas. It was the section of town where *turistas* were warned never to go.

Melanie parked, and she and Lassiter got out to walk down a spooky little alley that opened onto another street only slightly less disreputable than the first.

They entered a cantina, and the man behind the bar gave Lassiter a nod. *"¿Qué pasa, mi amigo?"* His gaze slid to Melanie and he grinned. *"Ella no es su tipo usual, Lassiter. Su gusto mejora."*

Lassiter said nothing as he led Melanie through a back door to the patio, but she had to wonder at the bartender's comment. If she wasn't Lassiter's type, then who was? And how many other women had he brought to this joint?

A few bleary-eyed patrons were scattered about the patio out back, but they paid scant attention to Melanie and Lassiter. It wasn't the kind of place where people noticed strangers. Or asked questions. Everyone kept to themselves, which was undoubtedly why Lassiter had chosen it.

They found a table in an isolated corner and sat down. A waitress with long black hair and a heavily made-up face ambled over to take their orders. When she leaned over the table, her breasts almost spilled out of the low-cut top she wore.

"What can I get for you?" she asked Melanie in English.

"Just a soft drink. It doesn't matter what kind."

The waitress turned with a seductive smile for Lassiter. "*¿Y para usted, señor?*"

"*Tequila, por favor.*"

Her smile lingered knowingly as she turned and sashayed off. She walked as if she were on a runway, one red spike heel placed in front of the other to maximize the sway of her hips.

Lassiter watched her until she was out of sight, then turned back to Melanie.

She pretended not to notice his interest in the woman just as she refused to acknowledge the unpleasant taste in her mouth that might have been jealousy.

Instead, she leaned toward him and asked almost angrily, "How do I know it wasn't you in my room earlier?"

His expression hardened. "Because I'm telling you it wasn't."

"Why should I believe you? If you were a man I could trust, you would have told me the truth last night. You wouldn't have threatened and coerced information from me that you obviously already had."

He leaned toward her, too, his eyes burning into hers. "I'm not going to apologize for last night. I needed information and I got it in the most efficient way I knew how. You're the only other person I know who can do what we do. I had to find out what you knew because all this time, I thought I was the only one..." He trailed off and settled back in his chair as the waitress brought their drinks. He didn't seem to notice the woman this time even though she made a production of bending over the table to place the glasses before them. When Lassiter failed to respond, the waitress shot Melanie a hostile look.

He waited until she was gone, then picked up his drink. "Look, you told me you don't really know how you do it. Well, I don't know, either. I assumed it was the result of an accident I was involved in, but seeing you in the infirmary the other night changed everything."

"What accident?" she said with a frown.

"We'll get to that in a moment. But if what you say about a doorway in your room this afternoon is true, it appears there may be someone else here in Santa Elena with our ability. And that person didn't come to your room out of mere curiosity. Someone is keeping tabs on you."

"But who?" she asked in a voice that sounded far more frightened than she would have liked.

"I guess that's what we have to find out."

She gazed at him across the table. "We?"

"Do you really want to go it alone, Melanie?"

She hesitated. "I'm not sure what I want anymore. I thought if I could find my father, everything would be all right somehow. All my questions would be answered. But it's not going to be that easy, is it."

"Nothing is ever easy," he said, and the look in his eyes made Melanie shiver.

"Tell me about the accident," she said softly.

His gaze dropped to his drink. "Do you remember

what happened to the Russian submarine, the *Kursk?*''

''There was some kind of explosion or collision,'' Melanie said. ''The crew was trapped for days. By the time the rescue team got there, it was too late. Everyone on board was dead.''

If possible, Lassiter's expression turned even darker. ''Five years ago there was a similar accident involving an American sub. No one knew about it because the incident was kept out of the media. Even the rescue efforts were secret.''

''Why?''

''In addition to the regular crew, there was a special-forces team on board. Their assignment was so top secret that for security reasons they were to be briefed on the specifics of the mission only after they were en route to the destination.''

Melanie frowned as she toyed with her drink. ''How do you know all this?''

''I was a member of that special-forces team.'' Their gazes met across the table and he nodded absently. ''There was some kind of explosion on the sub, but I never learned the cause. We lost power and crash-dove to the bottom of the North Atlantic. We were trapped more than three hundred feet below the surface.''

He raised his glass, and in one fluid move, drained the tequila. He immediately signaled the waitress for another. ''Because of the covert nature of my team's mission, we were kept isolated from the crew. Most of us escaped the brunt of the explosion because of where our quarters were located, but we were trapped inside. The hatches were all sealed. We could hear men screaming outside, but we couldn't get to them. We were in pitch-black until the emergency generators kicked in, but even then, the light was so dull we needed flashlights to ascertain the damage. And to make matters worse, we were listing so badly some of the men became disoriented.''

He paused again as the waitress brought his fresh drink. This time, she didn't bother practicing her feminine wiles on him. She plunked the glass on the table and hurried off to find a more appreciative audience.

''The loss of power meant that we had to contend very quickly with carbon dioxide,'' he said. ''And, of course, the cold. The residual heat didn't last long and hypothermia set in. Then fear, panic, isolation. And as the days wore on, helplessness.''

An unnatural claustrophobia clawed at Melanie's throat as she watched Lassiter's face. He remained expressionless, but there was something in his eyes, a shadow of the horror he'd been through…

She shuddered and tried to look away.

''The rescue efforts took days to coordinate and carry out. Everything had to be kept secret. By the time the divers and equipment reached the sub, everyone on board was dead.''

Melanie could feel the blood drain from her face. ''But…how could that be? You were there.''

His gaze lifted to hers. ''That's right. I was.''

Chapter Seven

"They got to our section first, but I don't know if that was by design or accident," Lassiter said. "The recovered bodies were taken aboard a military hospital ship equipped with a high-tech resuscitation facility. We were all flat line when they got us out. No pulse or heartbeat. No measurable blood pressure. No electrical activity in the brain. We were dead."

Melanie put a hand to her mouth, not knowing what to say. Her heart was beating a painful tattoo inside her chest. She didn't know why, but she was suddenly having trouble breathing.

"I was told later that the hypothermia dramatically slowed the rate at which postmortem cell deterioration took place," Lassiter said. "Otherwise, there would have been no hope. I don't remember any of this, of course, but at some point, I was given massive doses of epinephrine. An exsanguination needle was inserted into a vein and a bypass machine drew all the blood out of my body, warmed it, then pumped it back in."

Melanie shivered again. She couldn't help herself. "Were you the only survivor?"

"No, I don't think so. I know the others in my team were brought aboard the ship and later transferred to a hospital in Virginia at the same time I was. But I never saw them or talked to them. I was kept isolated. After I physically recovered, I went through weeks of debriefing. I don't remember a lot of it. What I do recall is that the day I was released from the hospital was the same day I was told I'd been discharged from the military as mentally unfit to serve."

Melanie stared at him in shock. "Like the *Eldridge* crew."

He nodded. "I was told in no uncertain terms that it would be a mistake to try and fight it. Or to even ask questions. For the sake of national security, I was to forget I'd ever been aboard that sub."

"What did you do after you left the hospital?"

"I drifted for a while," he said with a shrug. "There was really no place for me to go. Or so I thought."

Melanie frowned. "But you had a life before you entered the military. Why didn't you just go home?"

A shadow flickered across his features. "I grew up on a farm in the Mississippi Delta. My father died when I was just a kid, and my mother raised me. She and I were fairly close, I guess, but after I left the hospital, I knew I couldn't go back there. I was afraid my being there would somehow put her in danger, give them leverage to use against me. Besides…that part of my life was over. The memories of my mother belonged to someone else. The life I knew in Mississippi belonged to someone else. I couldn't go back.''

"How did you end up in Santa Elena?''

"I met a man in a bar one night. He was a mercenary who had contacts all over Central America. He needed someone for a job in El Salvador and I hired on. I've been in this part of the world ever since.''

"And the phasing?'' she asked carefully.

"I didn't know about it until I got down here. When it happened, I thought it had to be a phenomenon caused by the accident. When I died on that sub, I crossed over into another plane of existence or something. When I was resuscitated, I brought back with me the ability to move from one plane to another. Or at least, that's what I thought.''

"That's as good an explanation as any, I guess,'' Melanie murmured.

"That's what I told myself. But after I heard your story last night, I'm not so certain anymore. Maybe I was on that sub because of what I could already do.''

Melanie glanced up at him. "You don't remember anything about the mission?''

"The accident occurred before we were briefed.''

"What about before the accident? Your training? Other missions? You must remember something.''

He shook his head. "I have memories, but they're…vague. It's hard to explain.'' He glanced down at his hands. "Do you remember what you said last night about a special-ops team of super soldiers?"

"Are you telling me you think you were at Montauk?" When he didn't reply, Melanie said, "But you have memories of your childhood. You weren't abducted."

"I'm not so sure," he said grimly. "If they can engineer realities, what's to keep them from giving us false memories?"

He was right. Of course, he was right. It seemed as if "they" could do anything. "Why are you called *el guerrero del demonio?*" she asked. "Did someone see you phase?"

"Yeah. I ran into some trouble a year or so ago in Guatemala. My team was hired to take out the compound of a local drug lord. Someone sold us out and we were ambushed. The ones who weren't murdered were thrown in prison and tortured. I got out and came back for the others. A couple of them saw me go through a wall. They were grateful for the rescue, but they were also frightened. After that—" he lifted his drink "—the rumors spread. There were men who wouldn't work with me, and the contracts eventually dried up. Then a few months ago, Hoyt Kruger called me from his headquarters in Houston with an offer."

"From Houston? My father moved there after I went missing, but I suppose that's just a coincidence," Melanie said. "There couldn't be a connection, could there?"

"It's possible, I guess." Lassiter's curious gaze moved over her. "What do you remember about your father, anyway?"

"Hardly anything. I have memories of things he said to me and things we did together. But I can't put a face or voice with any of those memories."

"You must have seen photographs of him."

"Only a snapshot and it wasn't very clear. It was a group photo taken with his unit in Vietnam. I looked for it after my mother died, but I couldn't find it."

"Your father was in Vietnam?" His voice sharpened. "Do you remember if he had a tattoo on his upper left arm?"

"I have no idea. Why?"

"Angus Bond told me that Kruger's partner, a man named Martin Grace, has a tattoo on his arm similar to one he saw on a patient he treated in Vietnam. The wounded soldier was supposedly with a covert special-ops team. And he knew about the doorways."

"So Bond knows?"

"I don't think so. He didn't seem to understand what the man was talking about, but even so, the meeting and the tattoo made an impression."

Melanie frowned. "So you think my father had some kind of connection with these men?"

"I think there may be a *Vietnam* connection. Your father, Martin Grace, Hoyt Kruger. They're all around the same age, I would guess. So is Angus

Bond, for that matter. And they were all in Vietnam.''

"That doesn't mean they knew each other."

"But there's more. I told you earlier about a sniper who killed one of my men yesterday. I found the gunman's rifle after the shooting. It was the same kind of weapon that was used by snipers in Vietnam. I think he left it behind on purpose—as a warning. Taglio and I were standing only a foot apart. It could just as easily have been me in the sniper's crosshairs. I think he wanted to show me he could get to me when and wherever he chooses."

"And you think one of these men was that sniper?"

"I think it's very possible."

Melanie thought about that for a moment. "But why warn you?" she asked in confusion. "Why didn't he just take you out when he had the chance? If the Montauk people, or whoever we're dealing with, didn't want you talking about the accident or asking the wrong questions, why did they let you go in the first place? Why did they let *me* go? After they were through with us, why didn't they just…get rid of us?" '

"Because the people who are running this thing aren't soldiers, Melanie. They're scientists. And I have a feeling we're still their guinea pigs."

The nerves in her stomach tightened painfully. "Then whoever came to my room this afternoon wasn't just keeping tabs on my movements here in Santa Elena. They may have been watching me for

years. That's what you're trying to say, isn't it?''
Melanie glanced around the shadowy patio, wondering if someone was watching them at that very moment. When she'd returned home to her mother all those years ago, she hadn't been set free at all. She'd simply progressed to a new phase of experimentation. ''I feel sick,'' she whispered, the reality of the situation settling over her like a fetid smell.

Lassiter threw some bills on the table and stood. ''Come on. Let's get out of here.''

A few minutes later, they retraced their steps through the alley. Before they got to her vehicle, Lassiter took her arm and pulled her aside. ''I need to ask you something.''

''What is it?'' Melanie asked in alarm.

''What did you mean last night when you said you had a feeling the 'other side' was dangerous? Unstable, I think was how you put it.''

''It is,'' she said in surprise. ''It's one thing to go through a wall or a locked door, but I've always known that if I go too far or stay too long, the openings will close up. I won't be able to get out.''

He put his hands in his pockets as he gazed down at her. ''It's not like that for me.''

Her brows drew together. ''What do you mean?''

''There's no danger for me.''

''But…I don't understand.''

''I think I do. You were a little kid when they took you. Five years old, you said. They must have engineered a different reality for you because of your age. They might have been worried you'd wander too far, become disoriented and not be able to find your way back. Creating an unstable dimension, or the perception of one, was their way of keeping you on a short leash.''

Melanie leaned against the building and took a deep breath. For a moment, it felt as if a fist had closed around her heart. ''You know what, Lassiter? You were right. We're nothing but animals to these people. Two-legged lab rats. Haven't you ever wondered why we didn't ask questions? You said you were told not to, but I don't really see an oblique command like that stopping someone like you. Besides, you were leaving the military. You could do whatever you wanted. Why *didn't* you ask questions? Why didn't I?''

''Because we were programmed not to,'' he said.

She nodded, putting a hand to her mouth. ''They raped our minds, Lassiter. They used our worst fears against us. They stole our innocence and they turned us into something that doesn't feel quite human. And we let them because we were too young and frightened to fight them. We were like lambs being led to the slaughter. And now here we both are in Santa Elena, and I can't help wondering what happens now that we *are* asking questions.''

''I think that's fairly obvious,'' Lassiter said darkly. ''They'll try to stop us.''

''We can't let them. We have to find out the truth, because if we don't…'' Melanie squeezed her eyes closed as she brought her hands to her ears. ''I can still hear them screaming, you know. All those children…what they did to them…to us.'' She clenched her fists as she said fiercely, ''I hate them. I hate them for what they did to us. They had no right. They stole our childhoods, our minds, our free will…''

She was shaking so in her rage that Lassiter thought her legs might collapse out from under her. He didn't know what to say to her. How to calm her. He wasn't used to dealing with emotions. He'd shut out his own years ago.

Tentatively, he put a hand on her arm, and when she didn't pull away, he drew her to him. To his surprise, she melted against him, as if she hadn't had the offer of comfort in a very long time.

Her hands tangled in the front of his shirt. ''We have to stop them.''

''That won't be easy.''

''I don't care. I don't care…'' She buried her head in his shoulder, and he held her for a very long time.

MELANIE DIDN'T THINK she'd be able to sleep a wink that night knowing there might be someone other than Lassiter who could come in and out of her room at will. But if he was right and they were being watched—had been watched for years—changing hotels wouldn't help her. Even going back to the States wouldn't end the surveillance. All Melanie could do for now was try to find her father and pray he had some answers for her.

But there were no guarantees that he would. There were no guarantees that he was even still alive. He could have died years ago and whoever sent that last letter to Melanie's mother could have done so to lure Melanie to Santa Elena. But why? What could they do to her here that they couldn't have done to her back home? That they hadn't already done to her?

The more likely scenario was the one Lassiter had suggested the night before. Someone had followed her to Santa Elena in the hopes that she would lead them to her father. Because no matter how much she might wish it otherwise, Melanie couldn't help but believe that her father was in this thing up to his neck.

Shedding her clothes, she climbed into bed, prepared to spend the remainder of the night tossing and turning with an endless parade of questions marching through her head. But surprisingly she soon became drowsy. She closed her eyes as her mind began to drift, and just before she dozed off, she thought about the way Lassiter had held her earlier. Not tightly. Not seductively. Not with even a hint of passion. He'd held her as someone would hold a friend in distress.

But she and Lassiter weren't friends. They'd shared a moment of closeness and nothing more. The truer emotion had occurred between them earlier in his quarters, when he'd looked at her with heat in his eyes. When he'd pressed against her, letting her know how much he wanted her.

They were sexually attracted to each other. No point in calling it anything else. No point in trying to make more of it than it actually was.

They would sleep together and soon. The question for Melanie wasn't if but when.

Chapter Eight

When Melanie awoke the next morning, sunlight poured in through the French doors in her room. If someone had come in during the night, she hadn't seen him. If her belongings had been searched, she'd heard nothing. Her sleep had been undisturbed and surprisingly untroubled, given the nature of her thoughts before she'd drifted off.

She glanced at the bedside clock and noted that it was after eight. She was usually at the clinic by now, but Dr. Wilder had advised her to sleep in this morning. And after the conversation she'd overheard between him and Blanca the day before, Melanie wasn't all that keen on facing them.

Still, she'd have to go back eventually. Apart from her desire to spend time with Angel, she needed to go back to the clinic to see what else she could learn. There had to be a reason for Blanca's animosity and distrust, for her almost paranoid fear that Melanie would somehow bring them trouble.

And sometime during the night, Melanie had resolved to find out what that reason was.

After she showered and dressed, she quickly bandaged her wrist, then headed downstairs to the terrace to have breakfast. Several guests lingered over coffee, but none of them paid much notice as she took an unobtrusive table near the fountain. A man sitting alone two tables over nodded and smiled, then went back to reading his paper.

But all through breakfast, Melanie could feel his gaze on her, and once when she looked up, he stared at her openly. He was no longer smiling, and the way he watched her sent shivers up and down her spine.

In a strange way, he reminded her of Lassiter, but it had nothing to do with the man's appearance. Outwardly, he looked nothing like Lassiter, other than being about the same age and having a similar build. But there was something about his eyes, an intensity gleaming in those dark depths—and in Lassiter's— that had the power to chill her to the bone.

She quickly looked away, tried to concentrate on her breakfast, but it was impossible with him sitting so close. Staring at her so intently.

Who *was* he?

When Melanie glanced back in his direction, he was reading his paper again, but the damage had been done. She was completely unnerved.

Intent on leaving, she started to signal for the check, but unaccountably changed her mind. She sat back down and finished her coffee, determined not to let the stranger chase her off.

As she focused almost furiously on the distant scenery, her conversation with Lassiter the previous evening came rushing back to her. His account of the submarine accident had been so powerful that even in memory Melanie found herself breathless.

When she closed her eyes, she could almost feel the penetrating cold, the terrifying blackness, the claustrophobic reality of being trapped more than three hundred feet below the surface. The images were so powerful her heart started to hammer inside her chest. It all seemed so real to her.

The explosion followed by the screams…

The pandemonium as the submarine lost power and crashed to the bottom…

The cold…the darkness…the abject terror…

Once the vessel settled on its side, the crew's predicament would have become painfully clear. Panic would have set in, along with the numbing cold and the devastating realization that there was no way out.

Melanie could see it all, feel it all, and when her head cleared, she was trembling.

She glanced up, but the man who had been watching her earlier was gone. Whether he'd phased himself off the terrace or simply walked away, she had no idea.

Nor at that moment did she care. The vision she'd had of the doomed submarine had shaken her. Lassiter had been aboard that vessel. He'd experienced the horror she could only imagine.

But for one brief moment, she'd experienced it for herself. She'd been on board that sub with him.

And the terrible vision was like having a glimpse into Lassiter's dark, bleak soul.

Having seen it, Melanie knew her own life would never be the same.

LASSITER WAS ALONE in the mess tent when Kruger came in that morning. The older man filled a plate with lukewarm scrambled eggs, poured himself a cup of coffee, then made his way over to Lassiter's table. He didn't wait for an invitation, but sat down and began to eat, acknowledging Lassiter's presence with only a curt nod.

Light streaming in from the open sides of the tent gleamed off his bald head as he bent over his plate. Lassiter couldn't see his expression, but he knew there would be an enigmatic gleam in Kruger's blue eyes. There always was. Most people took it for humor, but Lassiter had come to believe that, more often than not, it was derision. Kruger was not the kind of man to tolerate fools.

There was a lot about him that Lassiter admired, but unfortunately, Kruger also had a side that Lassiter didn't completely trust.

Months ago, when they'd agreed on the terms of their arrangement, Lassiter had demanded and received a large payment up front, the bulk of which he'd placed in a numbered bank account in Aruba. But the outstanding balance due him when the operation was concluded would set him up for life. With that kind of money on the line, he wasn't about to take a chance on getting rolled. He'd had some of his contacts in the States check Kruger out, and they'd reported back to him that Kruger Petroleum was a solid company and a sound investment. But Kruger himself remained something of a mystery. No one seemed to know where he had come from or how he'd gotten his start in the oil business. Even industry insiders didn't know much about him, only that he had a formidable talent for making money.

The sleeves of his khaki shirt were rolled up past his elbows, and Lassiter caught a glimpse of a tattoo on his left arm. He couldn't make out what it was.

As if sensing his scrutiny, Kruger glanced up, his gaze narrowing. "Something on your mind, Lassiter?"

He shrugged. "Just finishing my coffee."

Kruger nodded absently, and they fell silent while he continued to eat. After a few moments, he looked up again. "What are you going to do about Taglio?"

"A local mortuary is picking up the body sometime this morning. He'll be buried this afternoon."

"I mean about replacing him. It's not a good time to be caught shorthanded. We've been hearing chatter about a major rebel offensive for weeks now. If the guerrillas are able to fracture the Cartégan army, they might decide to move in on my wells. And I don't have a lot of faith in *el presidente* and the ability of his generals to regroup and stop them. Those fat bastards will more than likely turn tail and run."

"I can get recruits," Lassiter said. "But it won't

be easy or cheap. And it may require me to be away from the compound for a day or two.''

Kruger took a sip of his coffee. ''You do what you have to do. The defense of this camp is in your hands.''

''I realize that. But I'm not here just to protect your wells. You also hired me to insure the safety of your crew. I told you weeks ago we need to have an evacuation plan in place—''

''And I told you we're not going anywhere,'' Kruger cut in. ''That's not how I operate. I'm not high-tailing it back to Houston just because things get a little dicey down here. Besides, I've been in worse places than this. A helluva lot worse.''

Lassiter took a stab in the dark. ''Like Vietnam?''

Kruger's gaze sharpened. ''Who told you I was in Vietnam?''

''I guess I heard it through the grapevine. I didn't know it was a secret.''

''It's not,'' Kruger said. ''But I don't like people nosing around in my private life. In fact, it really pisses me off.'' A shadow flickered across his features, something dark and cold and sinister. Something that made the hair on the back of Lassiter's neck stand on end. ''Vietnam was a long time ago. A lot of things happened there that I'm not proud of. But I've learned since I've gotten older that some things are best left buried in the past.'' His blue gaze regarded Lassiter across the table. ''The sooner a man accepts that, the better off he'll be.''

''GOOD. YOU GOT my message. Thanks for coming by.'' Angus Bond hauled a bottle of gin from his desk and filled a glass to the rim. "I wasn't sure you would."

"Why wouldn't I?" Lassiter asked with a shrug.

"You've got a lot on your plate these days, what with losing a man yesterday and all that talk about a rebel offensive. It's enough to drive a man to drink," Bond said cheerfully. He lifted the glass to his lips and took a long pull.

"You said it was urgent," Lassiter reminded him.

"So I did. Perhaps I exaggerated." Bond topped off his glass, then shoved the bottle aside. "I would offer you one of these, but I assume you're on duty."

"That's right. So if we could get to the point…?"

"And you never drink on duty, I'll wager. You're much too disciplined for that."

Lassiter tried to tamp down his impatience. "What did you need to see me about?"

"You're a man of discipline *and* principle. A rare combination these days."

Lassiter wondered how long Bond had been hitting the bottle. It wasn't yet ten o'clock, but the man's eyes were glazed, his speech slurred. "I think you've got the wrong man," Lassiter told him. "I've been called a lot of things in this part of the world, but principled isn't one of them."

"Maybe you have a lot of people fooled, then. But not me. I've known men like you before. In spite of your current circumstances, you have a code of honor by which you live your life. An ideology that you would fight and die for. And that, my friend, will be your downfall someday.''

"I fight for money these days," Lassiter said grimly. "And as for dying, I don't plan on doing that anytime soon. And besides, if I'm the kind of man you say, what am I doing in a hellhole like this?''

Bond shrugged. "Cartéga attracts its share of low-lifes, I'll grant you that. But not everyone who comes here is lawless, just as not every mercenary enjoys killing. I think you've found yourself in something of an awkward position, Lassiter. You're like a vampire with a soul, I suspect. You do what you have to in order to survive, but I rather think you might sometimes wonder if you'd be better off dead.''

Lassiter frowned. "You think you've got me pegged, do you?''

The older man laughed. "I doubt anyone has ever 'pegged' you. Not *el guerrero del demonio.*'' He leaned across the desk, his voice lowering conspiratorially. "What does a man have to do to earn such a nickname, anyway? From what I hear, you're good at what you do. Damn good. But a demon warrior would need to be more than just good, wouldn't he? One might even say he'd need to be more than human.''

"What are you getting at, Bond?''

The man shrugged as he took another sip of his gin, savoring the taste on his tongue before swallowing. "I've heard rumors about you, that's all. They say you have supernatural powers. You have the ability to become invisible, read minds, walk on water. Any truth to that?''

Lassiter gave a curt nod to the bottle on Bond's desk. ''How long have you been going at it this morning?''

Bond laughed again. ''Not long enough, Lassiter. It's never enough.'' The smile faded as he polished off the drink in one fluid move. He started to pour himself another, but then with grim resolve, screwed on the lid and slipped the bottle back into his desk. When he looked up, something in Lassiter's eyes made him grimace. ''I know what you're thinking. You're wondering how an educated, presumably intelligent man could end up like this. I still wonder that myself sometimes.''

''Your personal life is none of my business.'' Although Bond's drinking and drug use could very well affect everyone in the compound. But he worked directly for Kruger. There was nothing Lassiter could do about it.

''The thing is,'' Bond murmured, ''it happens so gradually you don't see it coming. And then one day you wake up in the gutter and you no longer have the strength or the desire to crawl out of it. So you just lie there wallowing in self-pity, waiting for the day when you don't wake up at all.''

He paused, his gaze still on Lassiter. ''It's a sorry excuse for a life, Lassiter. Doubly so when you still have memories of the way you once were. A man honored in his profession, respected in his community, loved and adored by his family. I once had it all. I was a man of principle, too. Or so I thought. And then just like that—'' he snapped his fingers ''—it was all taken away.''

''What happened?'' Lassiter asked in spite of himself.

Bond turned to stare out the window. ''Have you read much early American literature, Lassiter? I'm talking about the classics. Poe, Hawthorne, Melville.''

''Enough to get by in my high-school English classes, I guess. Why?''

''Hawthorne was always a favorite of mine. He had a recurring theme in much of his work. Man playing God. Science perverted by hubris. Let's just say, I can relate, if not sympathize, with his Dr. Rappaccini.''

''Look,'' Lassiter said, his patience finally exhausted. He had no idea where Bond was going with this conversation. ''If you're trying to tell me something, just spit it out. Otherwise, I don't have time for a reading assignment.''

Bond's gaze was slightly reproachful. ''I apologize for wasting your time, Lassiter. You have better things to do than listen to my sad tale.''

Guilt niggled at Lassiter, but he firmly shoved it aside. ''What do you want, Bond?''

''Your discretion, that's all. I'd like you to keep our conversation from yesterday privileged. I never should have said anything to you about Martin Grace. There's a matter of doctor-patient confidentiality involved here.''

"Telling me about a tattoo is hardly revealing classified medical information," Lassiter said.

"Still, it leaves me with a bad taste, and I'd rather you not repeat any portion of our conversation."

Too late for that, but Lassiter wasn't about to admit he'd already confided in Melanie. "Whatever you say."

"It's for the best." Bond glanced toward the door, as if suddenly worried someone might be eavesdropping. "You have to be careful what you say around here, Lassiter, and who you say it to. You can't trust anyone. Kruger is a fair man to work for, but you don't want to get on his bad side. He has a vicious temper. If you cross him, he'd just as soon slit your throat as look at you. And as for Martin Grace…let me put it this way." Bond's gaze darkened. "Kruger might slit your throat in a fit of rage, but I think Martin Grace would do it slowly. And I think he'd probably enjoy every minute of it."

Chapter Nine

Twilight had fallen by the time Melanie left the clinic that day. She'd purposefully put in extra hours hoping that by the time she departed, both Dr. Wilder and Blanca would have already gone home. She wanted to do a little snooping, try to find out why Blanca found her such a threat. And why Dr. Wilder felt the need to keep her close by.

But an emergency had kept everyone later than usual, and Melanie had finally been forced to leave first. To linger any longer would have been to invite suspicion, especially Blanca's.

Calling out her goodbyes to everyone, Melanie left by the front door and headed for downtown. Once she was a block or so away from the clinic, however, she skirted over a street and doubled back to the alley from which she'd observed Lassiter a few days ago. From there, she could watch the traffic to and from the clinic without being seen.

After twenty minutes or so, Blanca came out the front door and headed north, away from downtown.

Dr. Wilder followed a few moments later. Melanie didn't know exactly where he lived, but she'd heard one of the nurses mention that it was somewhere nearby. If an emergency arose during the night, he could be at the clinic in less than five minutes.

Melanie had no idea where Blanca lived, either, but she suspected the young nurse spent most of her evenings with Dr. Wilder. The woman's private life was certainly none of Melanie's business, but what did concern her was Blanca's attitude toward her and the secretive atmosphere in the clinic ever since she'd overheard that conversation.

Melanie couldn't shake the uneasy feeling that the secret Blanca and Dr. Wilder shared had something to do with her. And Blanca's animosity wasn't a simple matter of distrusting a stranger. It went deeper than that.

Melanie waited in the alley for another few minutes to make sure that neither Dr. Wilder nor Blanca returned. Satisfied they were both gone for the night, Melanie crossed the street and entered the clinic through the front door.

The nurse at the desk looked up in surprise. "*Hola,* Melanie. What are you doing here so late?"

"Hello, Elena. I left my bag," Melanie said with a rueful shrug. "My room key is in it, so I had to come back. All right if I go get it?"

Elena nodded. "No problem. But would you mind checking on Angel while you're back there? Blanca said she was a little restless earlier, and you always seem to have a calming effect on the child."

Melanie smiled. "I don't know about that, but I'll be happy to look in on her. I'll just let myself out the back door when I'm finished."

Elena nodded again, then returned to her reading as Melanie headed down the corridor. She peeked in on Angel and saw that the child was sleeping peacefully. Not wanting to disturb her, Melanie quietly closed the door and tiptoed away.

She went first to the closet at the back of the clinic to retrieve the bag she'd purposefully left there earlier. Then she hurried up the hall to Dr. Wilder's office, keeping a wary eye on the front in case Elena decided to come back and check on her.

The door was locked as Melanie had known it would be, but that didn't present much of an obstacle. As she'd told Lassiter last night, phasing through walls and locked doors was no problem for her. She could do so easily enough, but it wasn't something she liked to do. It wasn't normal. It wasn't human. And therefore, it just might be something for which God would not forgive her.

But it was too late to worry about that now. Melanie could already feel the tingle of electricity, the shifting vibrations in her body that allowed her to flow almost wavelike from one dimension into another.

She'd always thought going through the doorways a little like walking through warm Jell-O. Not difficult, but not an altogether pleasant sensation, either. The initial resistance was the hardest because during that time, half in and half out, Melanie was fully aware of two separate and distinct planes of existence. She was part of both worlds but belonged to neither, and it was always that brief moment of suspension that she feared the most. It was there, trapped between the two dimensions, that she was afraid she might lose herself forever, that the essence of her humanity might dissolve into nothing.

But as always, she emerged unscathed on the other side of the wall. She took a moment to reorient herself, then glanced around the office.

She had no idea what she was looking for, of course.

Removing a penlight from her bag, she shone the beam around the room, letting it linger on the desk, then angling it slowly over the walls until she spotted the row of file cabinets that she remembered were to her right. She started with the desk and then, finding nothing there, went straight to the files, wincing at the loud screech as she pulled open a metal drawer.

Most of the names on the tabs were of Spanish and Mayan origin, and she didn't recognize any of them. Aguilar, Andres, Arias…

She closed the drawer and skipped over to the last cabinet, searching through the S's. Sanchez, Serrano, Soto, Stark…

Melanie's fingers flew by the tabs so quickly she had to backtrack, certain her eyes must have played a trick on her. But no. There it was. The familiar name scrawled in faded ink across the tab. Richard Stark.

Her heart pounding, she pulled the folder from the

drawer and scanned the contents. The medical reports were all written in Spanish. Melanie's language skills were sufficient to get by in everyday situations, but reading medical or technical jargon was a different matter entirely.

She carried the folder to the desk and tried to make sense of the report, but before she had time to painstakingly work out the translation, loud voices in the hallway brought her head up with a start. Closing the folder, she hurried across the room and opened the door just wide enough to peer out.

Three men she'd never seen before strode down the hallway toward her. They were dressed in camouflage gear, which made her instantly think of Lassiter. And then of soldiers. Were they looking for her? Had Elena seen her go into Dr. Wilder's office and reported her?

Melanie started to panic, but then she saw that one of the men was injured. He was covered in blood and filth and leaning heavily on his companions, as if unable to stand on his own. The others were heavily armed and spoke rapidly in a dialect with which she was unfamiliar. She could only make out a word here and there as Elena shepherded them down the hallway.

The young nurse used soothing tones, as if trying to calm or placate them, but Melanie could detect an undercurrent of fear in her voice. She ushered them into a room at the back of the clinic, closed the door softly behind them, and then rushed back up the hall to the front of the clinic.

Satisfied that she hadn't been found out, Melanie closed the door and turned. And gasped in shock. Someone stood directly behind her.

A hand clamped over her mouth, and Melanie's first instinct was to struggle against the hold even though she almost immediately recognized Lassiter.

He put a finger to his lips and she nodded.

"What are you doing here?" she whispered furiously when he removed his hand.

"Looking for you."

"Did you feel it necessary to sneak up on me like that?"

He took her arm and pulled her away from the door. "Do you really want to have this conversation here?" he asked against her ear.

She smoothed clammy palms down her jeans, trying to calm her racing heart. But it wasn't fear that caused her shortness of breath. It was the man. It was his nearness. It was the way he made her feel. Like she was trapped on a crazy Ferris wheel that had suddenly spun wildly out of control.

"We need to get out of here," he said. "Those men are dangerous."

Her gaze shot to his. "You know them?"

"They're rebels. One of them was wounded earlier today when they ambushed an army convoy. The nurse has gone to call Dr. Wilder."

"Rebels?" Melanie repeated in surprise.

Lassiter nodded, his expression grim. "If your Dr. Wilder is caught aiding and abetting, he could be thrown in prison or even executed. I don't think it's a good idea for us to wait around here for the Cartégan Army to come looking for these guys.''

''Oh, my God,'' Melanie breathed. ''Then that explains why Blanca is so anxious to get rid of me. And why she feels so threatened by me. She's been worried all along that I'll find out what they're doing here.''

''I don't know anything about that,'' Lassiter said, ''but I repeat. We need to get out of here. *Now.*''

He took her arm, but Melanie shook him off. ''Lassiter, wait a minute. I think I've found something important.'' She hurried over to the desk and held up the folder. When he joined her, she shone the penlight on the tab. ''This file has my father's name on it. He must have been a patient here at some point.''

Lassiter frowned. ''Have you read it?''

''I tried but the medical terms are a little beyond my ability. How's your Spanish?'' She didn't really need to ask because she'd heard him that day in the old woman's shop when he'd followed her. Melanie knew he was fluent. Just one of his many talents, she suspected.

He took the folder and rummaged through the reports while she held the light for him. ''The date on this file is from ten years ago. Kind of odd they'd keep something this old in here with what I assume are the more recent files.''

''What does it say?'' Melanie asked anxiously.

''He came in complaining of severe abdominal pains and was treated for acute appendicitis. Looks like he had to have emergency surgery.'' Lassiter turned a page and froze. Melanie saw something cross his face that made her catch her breath.

''What is it?''

He closed the folder. ''It doesn't matter. We have to get out of here.''

''Not until you tell me what you saw.'' When he didn't answer, Melanie took the folder and scanned through the pages herself. The official-looking document was stapled to the back of the medical report and this time she needed no translation.

Certificado de Muerte.

Certificate of Death.

ONCE THEY WERE safely away from the clinic, Lassiter found an outdoor café where they could sit and have a drink. Melanie had said nothing since they'd left Dr. Wilder's office. She looked as if the wind had been completely taken from her sails.

The waitress came by their table, and Lassiter ordered tequila for both of them. But when the shots arrived, Melanie slid hers across the table to him. ''No, thanks. I don't drink.''

''One won't kill you. It might help settle your nerves.''

She stared at the drink for a moment, then shook her head. ''I can't. I don't dare.'' Her gaze lifted. ''I haven't had anything stronger than coffee to drink since I left rehab ten years ago. And the only drugs I take are an occasional aspirin for headaches.''

Considering what had happened to her as a child,

Lassiter supposed a history of addiction wasn't surprising. But she seemed like such a strong-willed woman now that had he not known about her past, he would have had a hard time imagining her succumbing to such self-destructive habits.

But he did know about her past. He knew about the kidnapping, the missing memories, the screams she heard every night in her sleep. He knew about a mother who couldn't bear the truth of what had happened to her daughter so she'd swept those missing years under the rug. Pretended the abduction had never happened. And Melanie, the adolescent, the teenager and now the woman, had to cope in the best way she knew how. In the only way she knew how.

"Could I have a cup of hot tea, instead?"

"Sure, no problem." He motioned for the waitress.

When the tea arrived, Melanie cradled the cup between both hands. "I don't know why I feel this way," she said. "I didn't even know him."

Lassiter shrugged. "It's not surprising. He was your father."

She glanced up, an edge of defiance sharpening her features. "It's not that. I'm not the sentimental type. But I was counting on him for answers that would help me understand and would…I don't know, maybe even give me a little peace." She stared into her tea. "Now it just seems hopeless."

In the candlelight flickering between them, she suddenly looked young and vulnerable, but Lassiter knew she wouldn't have been pleased by his observation.

He tried to ignore the sudden stir of emotions that tightened his chest. How could he feel anything for her? He was empty inside. As dead as the cold remains of his comrades that still lay at the bottom of the ocean. Even Melanie Stark couldn't resurrect something that had been buried for that long and that deep.

And yet the way she looked tonight, with candle-light dancing in her eyes...

Lassiter drew a deep breath, steadying himself. "We don't even know for sure that your father *is* dead."

Melanie looked up with a frown. "But you saw the death certificate. It looked pretty damn official to me."

"Death certificates can be faked." Lassiter leaned toward her. "Think about it, Melanie. Your father was on the run. He changed his appearance, his identity. What better way to disappear for good than to have the people who were looking for him believe him dead?"

"But if that were the case, he took an awfully big risk by writing that last letter to my mother. By asking me to come down here and meet him. He must have known there was a chance they'd follow me. Even after this long. Why would he take such a risk?"

"Because you're his daughter."

She gave him a look. "Don't delude yourself into

thinking he harbored some great love for me all these years. I still think he was involved in my kidnapping. When he couldn't face what he'd done, he took the coward's way out and left. All those years, he could have written to me. He could have come back to see me, but he didn't. So why *now?*''

Lassiter picked up his drink. ''I can't answer that. There's only one person who can. But I don't think it's a good idea to condemn a man unless you know his side of things.''

His defense drew an angry scowl across her face, but behind the cynical facade, Lassiter saw something else. A glimmer of hope. And suddenly he understood.

For years, Melanie had managed to convince herself that her father was the enemy. She'd had to in order to deal with his betrayal and abandonment. But a part of her had always harbored the hope that when she finally found him, he'd somehow turn out to be the father she'd always wanted and needed.

She glanced away, as if not wanting him to see what was in her eyes, let alone in her heart. ''I still say if he faked his own death, he wouldn't have risked exposing his new identity by contacting my mother.''

''There's always a chance he wasn't the one who faked the death certificate,'' Lassiter said. ''It still strikes me as a little suspicious that a ten-year-old medical report—on a foreigner, no less—would still be conveniently filed in Dr. Wilder's office.''

''Meaning?''

"Meaning someone could have put it there recently for you to find."

"Like who?"

"Someone who doesn't want a reunion between you and your father to take place. If you thought he was dead, maybe you'd give up searching for answers and go back home."

Melanie shoved a lock of hair behind one ear. "But how could they be so sure I'd find that file? How could they know I'd go there tonight looking for it?"

"Because they know you." Lassiter lowered his voice as he glanced around the terrace. They were seated away from the crowd, but he couldn't be sure of who might be listening in. He couldn't be sure if one of the nearby tourists was in fact an operative sent to keep tabs on them. "If we're right about these people, they've been watching you for over twenty years. They know your darkest secrets. Your deepest fears. They know everything about you because they've been inside your head. Given all that, it wouldn't be so hard to figure out what you'd do."

Melanie shuddered violently.

"I'm not trying to freak you out," he said. "I'm just reminding you that you can't believe everything you see or hear. Or read, for that matter. Reality is merely an illusion, remember?"

She closed her eyes briefly. "I know. But in some ways, it would be easier to believe that he really is dead. At least that would explain why he never came back. And why there was a gap in his letters. He and my mother corresponded all during the time I was missing and for several years afterward. But then the letters stopped for ten years. The last one arrived just weeks before my mother died.''

''How did she die?'' Lassiter asked carefully. ''I don't think I've heard you say.''

''She had a heart attack.''

''Sudden?''

''Yes.'' Lassiter saw the implication of his question hit her. She put a hand to her mouth. ''Oh, my God. Lassiter, what if they killed her? What if they gave her some kind of drug to make it look as if she'd died of natural causes? You said it yourself. We can't trust what we see or hear. Or what people tell us. They must have known that as long as my mother was alive, I'd never come looking for my father. But with her dead...''

''Melanie—''

''No, Lassiter, listen for a minute. They planted the letter in my mother's house knowing that I would be the one to go through her personal belongings. Don't you see? They killed her to get to me. They wanted me down here for a reason. And they wanted you here, too. It's not a coincidence that we both ended up in Santa Elena. It can't be. We're connected somehow.''

Their gazes locked across the table, and in spite of the seriousness of their discussion, something warm and electric passed between them.

Lassiter didn't want to feel anything for her. The last thing he needed was to become involved with

Melanie Stark who, if anything, carried around more baggage than he did. But like it or not, she was the most intriguing woman he'd met in years. And this thing between them…he couldn't remember a time when his attraction to a woman had been so intense. It was an adrenaline rush every time she looked at him.

She felt it, too. He could tell by the way her gaze suddenly darted from his, as if she'd seen something in his eyes she wasn't quite ready to face.

"Why us?" she asked almost desperately.

He thought she was referring to their attraction at first, but then he realized she'd gone back to their previous conversation.

"From what I've read, dozens if not hundreds of people were experimented on at Montauk. Why did they want the two of us here?"

"I think you've got it all wrong," Lassiter said slowly. "I don't think they did want us here. Not together, at least. These people operate in shadows, and they can't risk having their activities exposed. As long as they keep us isolated and under control, they have nothing to fear. But once we start asking questions, make no mistake, Melanie, they'll do whatever they have to do to stop us."

Chapter Ten

Doubt flickered in Melanie's eyes. "So you're saying our being here in Santa Elena at the same time *is* just a coincidence?"

"I don't believe in coincidences," Lassiter said. "We were brought here for a reason, all right, but the Montauk people had nothing to do with it."

"Then who brought us here? And why?" When he didn't answer, Melanie's eyes widened. "You really do think my father is still alive, don't you. You think he's the one who arranged all this."

"I don't know," Lassiter replied truthfully.

She stared off into the distance. Light danced across her features, casting an intriguing mix of light and shadow, like the woman herself. "You told me last night that you think the sniper who killed one of your men had been sent here to warn you. Or to stop you. And you think he's one of a group of men, including my father, who served together in Vietnam."

"It's only a hunch."

"I know. But those men you mentioned last night—Hoyt Kruger, Martin Grace, Angus Bond." Her gaze came back to his. "What if they aren't just connected to my father, Lassiter? What if one of them *is* my father?"

He'd thought about the possibility himself, especially after his strange talk with Angus Bond earlier. "You've met Bond," he said. "Did you recognize him?"

"No, not really. But there was something familiar about him," she admitted. "Something in his eyes that I've seen before. But I don't think it was recognition. Not in the way you mean."

"Do you know anything about the works of Nathaniel Hawthorne?" he asked suddenly.

"Nathaniel Hawthorne?" Melanie's brows lifted in surprise. "Whoa. Where did that come from?"

"Do you?"

She shrugged. "I read *The Scarlet Letter* in high school. Why?"

"I had a talk with Bond today. He was in a strange mood. He seemed to want to tell me something— about his past, I think—but then he started rambling on about a recurring theme in Hawthorne's writing. Man playing God. Science corrupted by hubris. He compared himself to someone named Rappaccini."

Melanie stared at him for a moment. "Are you sure he said Rappaccini?"

"Yeah, I'm sure. Do you know what he was talking about?"

She leaned forward, her eyes gleaming with excitement. "Lassiter, 'Rappaccini's Daughter' is one of Hawthorne's short stories. It's about a man who was willing to sacrifice his own daughter for the sake of his science."

Lassiter sat back in his chair. "Well," he said. "Maybe Bond really was trying to tell me something."

"Like the fact that he's my father?" Melanie bit her lip. "But he can't be. My father wasn't Australian."

"How do you know? You said you didn't remember anything about him, not even the sound of his voice. Besides, accents can be faked just like death certificates."

"My God, Lassiter. How are we supposed to make sense of this? It's like a dream. Nothing is real. I don't know what to believe anymore. I don't know who I can trust."

Lassiter waited a heartbeat, then said, "Maybe it's time we started trusting each other."

Her gaze dropped. "I don't know if I can do that. I don't know if I want to trust you."

"Why not?"

"Because the last person I ever truly trusted was my father. And look what he did to me."

THEY LEFT THE CAFÉ and headed toward Melanie's hotel. As they neared the plaza, the streets came alive with music and laughter from the restaurants and cantinas, but the sound did little to assuage Melanie's growing fear that she was being constantly monitored. Her every move watched by unseen eyes. Her every thought analyzed to be used against her. She couldn't shake the notion that nothing was as it seemed and never had been.

She glanced at Lassiter. Could she trust him? She wasn't at all certain she would ever be able to trust anyone again, but she remembered something she'd learned years ago in rehab. Take small steps and take them one at a time.

So she kept on walking beside him. And after a while, she felt some of her uneasiness slip away.

"When I told you earlier that I'd been in rehab, you didn't show much reaction," she said. "Don't you want to ask me about it?"

Lassiter shrugged. "It's none of my business. If you want to talk about it, fine. I'll listen. But you don't owe me any explanations. And you don't have to justify yourself to me."

"I wasn't going to do that." She sounded a little defensive. "But I thought you should know that it's all behind me. I'm a different person now. If we find ourselves in a tough situation, you can count on me. I won't fall to pieces."

He almost smiled at that. "You'd be about the last person I'd expect to fall to pieces."

"Don't give me too much credit," she said. "I've hit rock bottom more times than I care to remember. There was a time when no one could count on me, including myself."

"People change."

"People change? That's all you have to say about

it? Lassiter, are you telling me you don't have even
the slightest bit of curiosity about what I did back
then? About the kind of person I was?''

"No," he said. "I don't."

Melanie didn't quite know how to take his answer.
The men who had come and gone from her life had
all said they didn't care about her past, but when
push came to shove, they did. And somehow it always came back to haunt her. To hurt her. "You
don't care because you don't care about me or because…you accept me for who I am?'' To Melanie's
surprise, her heart had started to pound against her
rib cage. So hard it was almost painful. Which was
strange. It wasn't as if his answer mattered to her or
anything.

He stopped walking and turned to her. "You really
want to know what I think of you?''

She nodded and swallowed, bracing herself for the
truth. And for just a moment, his face blurred and
she saw Andrew staring down at her. *What I see
when I look into your eyes scares the hell out of me,
Mel.*

"I think you're a survivor, just like me."

She gave a shaky laugh. "It's good to know we
have something in common, I guess."

"We have more than that in common, and you
know it."

A tremor coursed through Melanie at what she saw
in Lassiter's eyes. It was the same thing she'd seen
back at the café. The same thing she'd seen in his
quarters the night before.

Melanie was no stranger to passion, but somehow she knew with Lassiter it would be different…and possibly devastating.

''I'm not sure I'm ready for this,'' she murmured.

''Only one way to find out.'' He wove his hands in her hair and lowered his head to kiss her.

The heat between them was immediate, intense and completely overwhelming. Melanie's eyes fluttered closed as her breath caught in her throat. She wanted Lassiter, had wanted him from the moment she first laid eyes on him, more than she'd ever wanted any man.

He walked her back into the shadows as she wound her arms around his neck and kissed him back. Kissed him with a dark, urgent hunger that shocked and thrilled and scared her all at the same time. She kissed him as if her very life depended on it.

And Lassiter responded just as she'd hoped he would. He ground his body against hers as his tongue savaged her mouth. His hands slipped inside her shirt and moved up her back, sending hot and cold chills up her spine. Then slowly he slid his hands down her sides, letting his thumbs play over her breasts with a hot, sure touch that drew a violent shiver from somewhere deep inside her.

Melanie curled one leg around his as her hand moved to the front of his jeans.

He pulled away, breathing hard as he buried his lips in her neck. ''Are you sure? Someone could see us here.''

She drew his mouth back to hers. "I don't care," she whispered. "I don't care, I don't care, I don't care."

THEY KISSED in the elevator all the way up to her room. They kissed while Melanie clumsily inserted the key into the lock and opened the door. And then, staggering inside, Lassiter kicked the door closed behind them as he hauled her up against the wall and kissed her some more.

Melanie was on fire by this time. She slid her hands up his arms, over his shoulders, across his chest, reveling in the hard ripple of his muscles. He was in terrific shape, which certainly seemed to bode well for the next several minutes of what she fervently hoped would be an intense physical workout.

He finally tore his mouth from hers and stepped back long enough to rip her tank top over her head and then to do the same with his own shirt. By the time he was finished, Melanie had struggled out of her jeans and kicked them aside.

"You're very efficient," he muttered, pressing up against her. "I admire that in a woman."

"I know what I want," she whispered, dragging his mouth down to hers. "And I'm not afraid to go after it." She kissed him then in a way that drew a deep, masculine, thoroughly erotic groan from his throat.

When he pulled her into his arms, Melanie went with open eyes and an open mind. When he lifted her off the floor, she locked her legs around him tightly.

"Easy, baby. Give me some room to maneuver," he muttered.

"Sorry." She placed her hands on either side of his face, kissing his eyelids, his nose and finally his mouth as he fumbled with the zipper of his jeans. By the time he stumbled back to the bed, he was already inside her.

He sat on the edge with Melanie draped around him, moving so frantically at first that he grasped her hips to slow her. When he lay back on the bed, he pulled her down with him, capturing her breasts with his hands and then his mouth, sending thrill after thrill spurting through her bloodstream.

"Man, you're good at this," she gasped.

"Am I?"

"You can't tell?"

"You do seem pretty turned on," he said appreciatively.

"Yeah. And Siberia is pretty cold in the winter."

The truth was, Melanie had been close to the edge ever since they'd first kissed on the street. Dangerously close. Scarily close. And then, when he'd gone all he-man and ripped off his shirt, exposing all that beautiful tanned skin and those glorious muscles...

She sighed in ecstasy. She didn't like to think of herself as the shallow type. She'd been attracted to men in the past for all kinds of reasons. But Lassiter...well, there was just no point in lying to herself about it. He was one seriously hot guy. All she had to do was *look* at him.

But she was doing more than looking, and so was he. His hands were all over her, finding all kinds of erotic little places.

"Hey, be careful there," she murmured.

He gazed up at her with smoldering eyes. "Why's that?"

"One wrong move…or should I say one *right* move…"

"Then you'd better hold on." He gave her a look that ratcheted up her blood pressure another notch or two. "Because this is about to get interesting."

"Interesting, I can handle. It's what you were doing before…oh, God…"

Still entwined, they rolled, until Lassiter was staring down at her, his gaze dark, deep and blazing hot. "You are one gorgeous woman," he said almost reverently.

The tone of his voice rattled her for a moment. "Ditto," she said breathlessly. "I mean, about the gorgeous part. Obviously, you're not a woman." Her eyes widened. "Obviously."

And then as he began to move inside her, the earth moved around her. Melanie closed her eyes, giving herself up to a pleasure so intense it was almost painful.

LASSITER WAS NOT the kind of guy to linger in the afterglow. He rose in the darkness and grabbed his clothes from the floor, dressing with a quick efficiency that might lead one to conclude he was no stranger to hasty exits.

Melanie lay naked on the bed, curled around a pillow, as she watched him. "You don't have to hurry off on my account, you know. I'm not the kind of girl who expects dinner and a movie afterward."

He pulled on his jeans and snapped them. "I've been gone from the compound a long time. I have to get back before someone misses me."

"Would I run you off even faster if I asked when I'll see you again?"

He sat down on the edge of the bed to put on his shoes. "Soon. I'll be in touch."

"Oh, I think I've heard that one before," she murmured.

He turned to glance at her, a shadow flickering across his features. "Not from me you haven't. And just for the record, I'm not running away. I do have to get back."

Melanie propped herself on her elbow. "It'd be okay if you were. I'd understand. I've done it myself."

"I'm not running away."

"I mean, it's not like we need to get all strange about it or anything. It was just sex. Great sex, but…sex, right?"

He was dressed now and he rose to stand over the bed. "I'm not running away," he said. "And if I were? It might be because it wasn't just sex. Did you ever think about that?''

LASSITER LEFT Melanie's room the normal way. He opened the door and slithered out into the hallway, like the snake that he was.

He hadn't lied when he said he had to get back to the compound. He did. But it wasn't imperative that he leave that second. He could have hung around for a few minutes and…what? Made small talk until they ended up making love again? And that was exactly where it would have led. No use kidding himself about that.

He paused in the hallway and frowned back at her door. Even now he had the strongest urge to go back inside and take her again if she'd let him. He couldn't get enough of her, and it wasn't just sex, no matter how hard she'd tried to convince him otherwise.

A casual encounter he could handle. He lived for meaningless sex.

But the problem was, if it had just been about sex, Lassiter was pretty sure he wouldn't be feeling as if the floor had just dropped out from under him.

ACTUALLY, MELANIE *had* considered the possibility that Lassiter's hasty departure had been triggered by more than his desire to escape an awkward moment. After all, he had to realize by now that she wasn't the kind of woman who needed assurances or empty promises. She knew the score. She'd been around the block a few times. She wasn't looking for anything permanent here, either, so why had he felt the need to run?

Because maybe, just maybe, she'd gotten to him in a way that frightened him. Just as he frightened her.

Sex was one thing. But an emotional commitment…that led to danger. That led to disappointment. That was not good.

But something had occurred to Melanie earlier as she'd lain in Lassiter's arms. Something she couldn't get out of her head now. Maybe their being in Santa Elena really wasn't a coincidence. Maybe someone—or something—had brought her and Lassiter here at the same time…because they were meant to be together.

MELANIE DREAMED she was on board the submarine that night. But she couldn't see Lassiter anywhere. She couldn't see anything, in fact. It was pitch-black where she was. And cold. So cold her body was going numb.

Somehow she knew that everyone else on board was dead. She was the last one, and she wanted nothing more than to find a soft place to curl up and join them.

But it wasn't yet time for her to die. She still had questions. She needed to live in order to find out the truth, but she couldn't seem to shake off her growing lethargy. She couldn't breathe. The air had run out.

Suddenly the dream changed. Melanie was no longer aboard the sub, but she still couldn't breathe. Something was pressing against her face, covering her mouth and nose, blocking her air…

Someone was trying to smother her!

Melanie fought her assailant with everything in her, and when she finally slung the pillow from her face, she bolted upright in bed, gasping for breath as her gaze darted around the darkened room.

She'd been certain her attacker would be hovering nearby, ready to pounce on her again before she could gather her strength.

But no one was there. She couldn't see so much as a glimmer of light that would have given away the presence of a doorway through which her assailant might have escaped.

It had been a dream, she thought in relief. A shrink might even conclude that the nightmare was directly related to her growing feelings for Lassiter and her rather claustrophobic fear of commitment.

Getting out of bed, she walked into the bathroom to splash cold water on her face. As she patted her skin dry, she glanced at her reflection. The woman in the mirror was the same one who always stared back at her. Same eyes. Same nose. Same mouth. But the problem was, Melanie had no idea who that woman was.

She dreaded the moment when Lassiter would look deep into her eyes and see nothing but the emptiness inside her.

As she started to turn away, she caught a glimpse of something in the mirror that caused her heart to jump. She could see into the bedroom, and for just a split second, a shadow moved just beyond the doorway.

Someone was there.

Frantic, Melanie glanced around for a weapon. Except for a can of hairspray, the bathroom contained nothing remotely deadly. If she had a match or a lighter, she might have been able to fashion a blowtorch the way Agent 007 had done in a movie. But Melanie didn't have a light, and this wasn't Hollywood. There wasn't even much hairspray left in the can. At best, she had one good shot at the intruder's eyes.

Padding silently across the floor, she glanced into the bedroom. She didn't see anything at first, but then, as her eyes adjusted to the darkness, she saw the telltale shimmer of light across the room near the French doors.

In the split second before the light faded completely, Melanie had the uncanny feeling that someone was watching her from the other side.

Chapter Eleven

The guard at the gate wouldn't allow her through, even though she'd worn her best skirt—a filmy affair with a side split that showed plenty of leg—and high-heeled sandals that were ridiculously inappropriate for jungle wear.

Melanie lifted her sunglasses so that the guard could see her blue eyes as she gave him a smile designed to make a young, virile man forget about duty, honor and country. And in his case, all he had to worry about was his job.

"Are you sure you can't let me in? Just for a few minutes? I won't stay long, I promise. I drove all the way from Santa Elena just to see him, and it would be such a shame if I didn't even get to say hello."

The guard's expression remained taciturn even though his gaze dipped appreciatively to her legs. "No one is allowed inside the compound without permission from Kruger. Sorry."

She sighed in discouragement. "Can you call him for me at least?"

Before the guard could answer, another car pulled up on the other side of the fence, and a tall, middle-aged man climbed out. He strode toward the gate, his bald head gleaming in the sunlight. "What's going on here?"

The guard stepped quickly away from Melanie's vehicle. He didn't salute the newcomer, but he very visibly came to attention. "Mr. Kruger," he said with more than a hint of deference. "I was just telling the young lady here that no one is allowed inside the compound without your permission."

The bald man's gaze fell on Melanie then, and a slight tremor slid up her backbone. He had a pleasant face, but there was something in his eyes, a hint of ruthlessness that made her think he was not a man to be trifled with. She didn't so much as bat her lashes at him as he approached her.

"I'm Hoyt Kruger," he said, extending his hand. "What can I do for you?"

Melanie placed her hand in his and felt something akin to an electrical shock surge along her nerve endings. It wasn't sexual tension or even attraction. It was something more disturbing. An odd sort of recognition even though she didn't think she'd ever met him before. Not that she could remember, anyway.

She managed a smile. "My name is Melanie Stark. I'm a friend of Dr. Bond's. I was hoping to see him today."

Kruger's brows lifted slightly in surprise. "*Angus* Bond? Amazing what an Aussie accent will get you."

Melanie laughed. "Do you think it would be possible for me to see him? If you don't want me inside the compound, perhaps he could come out here."

Kruger studied her for a moment longer, then said over his shoulder, "Open the gate." He turned back to Melanie. "Follow me. I'll try to help you find him."

"Thanks," Melanie said as she depressed the clutch, waiting for the guard to open the gate. Once Kruger had turned his vehicle around, she followed him into the heart of the compound.

It looked pretty much the way she remembered it. Long, sheet-metal buildings that served as bunkers. A cluster of smaller buildings that were used for the office, the infirmary and equipment storage. And in the distance, the constant drone of machinery as another hole was drilled hundreds of feet below the earth's surface.

Kruger stopped in front of her and shouted something to a man wearing orange coveralls and a hard hat. The man gestured over his shoulder.

Kruger got out of his vehicle and approached Melanie's. "I think you'll find Angus in the mess hall." He turned and pointed toward an open-sided tent near the infirmary. "I wouldn't stay too long, if I were you. We don't get many visitors out here. Not the kind who look like you, anyway. Some of the men are a little rough around the edges, so it's best not to tempt fate."

Melanie nodded. "I'll make it quick. Just long enough to say hello."

Kruger looked as if he wanted to say something else, but then changed his mind with a shrug. He strode back to his vehicle, climbed in and drove off without a backward glance.

Melanie parked and got out. The long tables and benches lined up beneath the mess tent were almost empty. She spotted Bond sitting alone at the far end, and as she walked toward him, he looked up suddenly, as if sensing her presence.

Shock flashed across his features.

"Hey, remember me?" she called out gaily.

He broke into a smile that, to his credit, seemed only a little strained. "Yes, of course. Melanie, isn't it? The woman who took pity on me the other afternoon so I wouldn't have to drink alone." He rose as she neared his table. "What brings you all the way out here? And how in the world did you get past the guard at the gate?"

"Actually, I came to see you," Melanie said. "And Mr. Kruger himself let me inside the compound."

Bond gave her a skeptical look. "You drove all the way out here to see me? I must say, I'm deeply flattered. But you'll forgive me if I have to ask why. Naturally, I'd like to think my charm, charisma and rugged good looks brought you out here, but, alas, I'm nothing if not a realist."

"Well, then, you just might be surprised," Melanie said with a smile. She liked the man. Whether he was her father or not, there was something about Angus Bond that had drawn her to him from the first.

"I'm here because I'm getting bored with my own company. My Spanish leaves a lot to be desired, so I haven't really met anyone in town. I kept hoping I'd run into you and I could buy you that drink I owe you. But when I didn't, I decided to take matters into my own hands. I hope you don't mind."

As if suddenly realizing they were still standing, he motioned for her to sit, his expression all the while one of bemusement. "Well, I must say, all that sounds perfectly reasonable. And I accept your offer of a drink. How about later today? Say six o'clock? Same place we met last time?"

"That'd be great."

"Good. Now that we have that issue out of the way, why don't you tell me why you're really here?"

Melanie's smile faltered. "Am I that transparent?"

"I'm afraid so."

"Then I'd better come clean, hadn't I." She leaned toward him and lowered her voice. "That man we saw in town the other day. The one you called Lassiter. What can you tell me about him?"

Bond frowned. "I can tell you the same thing I told you before. If I had a daughter, he'd be the last person on earth I'd want her to be alone with."

"May I ask why you feel that way?" Melanie tried to keep her voice neutral, but the very mention of Lassiter's name conjured up images she'd been trying to avoid all morning. His hard body against hers…his hands all over her…the way he moved when he—

"I can only assume your interest in him is because…you're interested in him," Bond said carefully. Something in his voice changed, but Melanie couldn't quite put her finger on what it was.

She gave an awkward laugh. "Again, I'm transparent. Okay, I'll admit it. My interest in him is purely superficial."

Bond sighed. "Why is it that women are always drawn to men like him? Is it the danger? It must be, because I suspect you have a bit of the wild child in you, as well," he accused. "I can see it in your eyes. You crave adventure and excitement, no matter the cost. And I also have a feeling that you are your own worst enemy."

His assessment was so dead-on that it made Melanie uneasy. "Wow," she tried to say lightly. "You figured all that out about me in the short time we've known one another?"

His gaze met hers. "It wasn't difficult. We're kindred spirits, I'm afraid. I knew it the moment I first saw you in town. That's why I came over to your table. I think you felt it, too."

Melanie's pulse quickened at his tone, at the shadows of regret that were suddenly in his eyes. Like Lassiter, she had the strongest feeling that Bond was trying to tell her something, and she wanted to blurt, *Just say it. Don't leave me hanging.*

He looked stricken. "Oh, dear. I hope I didn't give you the wrong impression."

"What do you mean?"

"I'm not trying to come on to you. Please don't think that."

Come on to her? That was the last thing she would have considered. "I don't think that."

"If anything, I feel…an avuncular connection to you."

Melanie's heart gave a painful jerk. "You…do?"

"Yes, of course. If I had a daughter, I imagine she'd be a lot like you."

If I had a daughter…

He *was* trying to tell her something.

Melanie had waited so long to hear him say it. She'd even dreamed about it on occasion. A nameless, faceless stranger coming to her in her sleep. His voice deep and rich and full of emotion. *"I'm your father, Melanie. I've loved you all these years. I've never stopped loving you, and I'm proud that you're my daughter."*

Well, she might as well continue to dream, Melanie told herself grimly. Because even if Angus Bond was her father, that didn't mean he loved her. That didn't mean he could be proud of the way she'd turned out.

"Are you all right?" he asked in concern. "You look a little pale."

"I'm fine. It's just…I get the feeling you're trying to tell me something."

The regret in his eyes deepened. "Yes, I guess I am."

"What is it?" she asked anxiously. "Please tell me."

He hesitated, his gaze slipping away from hers. "It's about Jon Lassiter. You have to be careful with a man like that. He's not to be taken lightly, Melanie, and he's certainly not to be trusted.''

She tried to swallow back her disappointment. ''You implied that before, but you've yet to tell me why.''

''It's obvious, isn't it? You're a young, beautiful woman traveling alone in a foreign country. If you go looking for trouble, I'm afraid you're apt to find it. And maybe when and where you least expect it.''

LASSITER COULDN'T believe his eyes. What was she doing here? And how the hell had she gotten past the guard?

The obvious answer was that she'd phased herself through the fence, in broad daylight.

Melanie Stark was a lot of things, but stupid she wasn't. Somehow she must have gained access to the compound in the conventional way or she wouldn't be sitting right out in the open, chatting up Angus Bond as if the two of them were long-lost friends.

Which brought Lassiter back to his original question. What the hell was she doing there?

He watched her from a distance, his mind flashing back, in spite of himself, to the evening before. The way she'd kissed him. The way she'd touched him. The way, as they'd walked back to the hotel, she'd been ready to go at it all hot and heavy with only shadows to protect them from prying eyes.

It had been his idea to go back to her room. Melanie had been impatient with what she considered a waste of time, but they'd put it to good use. And by the time they'd gotten to the hotel...*man*. She'd been a firecracker. Completely uninhibited. A woman who wasn't afraid to take a few risks. A lot of risks, actually.

She was a lot like him, Lassiter thought with a sudden frown. And that worried the hell out of him, because there was nothing more dangerous than a person who didn't have anything to lose.

He started toward her, then turned when he heard someone behind him call out his name. He saw Martin Grace hurrying from the office toward him. As usual, the man's demeanor was condescending and unpleasant, and Lassiter couldn't help remembering what Bond had said about Kruger and his partner. *Kruger might slit your throat in a fit of temper, but Martin Grace...I think he'd do it slowly. And I think he'd probably enjoy every minute of it.*

"I heard we had a visitor," Grace said, his gaze going past Lassiter to the table where Bond and Melanie still sat. "Get rid of her."

"I was just about to take care of it," Lassiter said.

Grace stared at Melanie for a moment longer, and before he finally turned away, Lassiter saw something disturbing in his eyes. It was a look he'd seen before, in the eyes of the Guatemalan prison guard whose job it had been to inflict torture on the prisoners. It was a job the man had relished.

"Escort her from the compound and make sure she doesn't come back," Grace barked. "Understand?"

Lassiter nodded. "She won't come back." He'd see to that.

ONCE THEY WERE out of range of the surveillance cameras, Lassiter pulled his vehicle to the side of the road and strode back to Melanie's rented four-wheel drive. "What the hell do you think you're doing coming out here dressed like that? Some of these guys have done some serious time, Melanie, for crimes you don't even want to think about. Trust me, you do not want to be the object of their fantasies."

His imperious tone immediately fired Melanie's temper, even though the sight of him in his camouflage, demon-warrior pants and tight green T-shirt sent her pulse racing. He was certainly inspiring *her* fantasies. "You know why I came. Last night we talked about a connection between those men and my father, and the possibility that one of them could even *be* my father. I wanted to see if I recognized any of them."

"Did you?" Lassiter still seemed distracted by the amount of leg showing through the slit in her skirt. He frowned, as if annoyed with himself for his lack of focus.

"I wouldn't say recognized, exactly. But, Lassiter, I see what you mean about Angus Bond. I think he's definitely trying to tell us something."

"What did he say?"

"He said if he had a daughter, he imagined she'd be a lot like me. And that we were kindred spirits, which was what drew him to me in the first place. That can't be a coincidence, can it? It's not just some throwaway remark. He was trying to tell me something."

"That he's your father, you mean?"

"Maybe. Or at least…that he knows about my father. I don't know." She threaded her hair behind her ears. "Maybe I was just hearing what I wanted to hear. He could be nothing more than a harmless drunk who's reaching out to me because he senses I'm a sympathetic listener."

"Did he say anything else?"

She gave him a sidelong glance. "Actually, he warned me about you, Lassiter. He said I shouldn't trust you."

When he didn't respond, Melanie said, "Well, aren't you going to dispute it?"

He hesitated for so long that she began to get nervous. "Lassiter?"

His gaze slid away. "Maybe he has a point."

Melanie didn't like the sound of that. She recognized a weasel answer when she heard one. "Why do I get the feeling that *you're* trying to tell me something?"

"No, it's not that—"

"Because if you're trying to tell me what I think you are," she cut in, "I'm going to be damned pissed. You were the one who said last night that we should start trusting each other. And now you're blowing me off?"

"I'm not blowing you off."

"Well, it sounds that way to me. You got me into bed. You got what you wanted, and now, suddenly, I'm not supposed to trust you?" She hit her palm against the steering wheel. "I don't *believe* this."

"It's not that way," he insisted.

"Then what way is it? Why has everything suddenly changed because we had sex?"

"Because it has," he said angrily. "Because you scare the hell out of me."

That took her aback for a moment. "*Why?* Why would someone like you be afraid of me?"

"Because I'm afraid of what I might be willing to do to have you."

The way he looked at her made Melanie's insides quiver. She let her head fall back against the seat as she stared up at him through hooded eyes. "You don't have to do anything to have me. I proved that last night, didn't I?"

"Last night only confirmed what I've been afraid of all along." Lassiter's voice was heavy with dread, raw with hunger. "Once I've had you, I won't be able to get enough of you."

He curled a hand around her ankle and slid it slowly up her leg. When he was under her skirt, Melanie put her hand over his, but not to stop him...

Chapter Twelve

"What do you mean, she's gone?"

"Ella se ha ido. Alguien vino y se la llevó lejos."

"Took her away where?" Melanie demanded.

The nurse shrugged as she efficiently went about the business of putting fresh linens on Angel's bed. "I don't know, *señorita*. You need to talk to the doctor."

"Is he in?"

The nurse cast an anxious glance over her shoulder. She was a young woman Melanie had never met before. "You can try his office."

"Thanks, I will." Melanie whirled and strode out the door and across the hallway to Dr. Wilder's office. She knocked once, then opened the door and stepped inside. Blanca, seated behind the desk, glanced up with a frown.

"Where's Dr. Wilder?" Melanie asked.

"He's not here."

"I can see that. Where is he?"

Blanca made no effort to hide her disdain. "Not

that it's any of your business, but he had to go to San Cristóbal for a few days.''

Melanie crossed to the desk. ''Does he know about Angel?''

''What about her?''

''One of the nurses told me that someone came and got her this morning. I want to know who it was and where they took her.''

''I don't have to tell you anything,'' Blanca said coldly. ''Angel's welfare doesn't concern you any longer.''

Melanie planted her hands on the desk. ''If you don't tell me where Angel is right this second, I swear to God, I'll…''

''You'll what?'' Blanca rose to her feet and tossed back her hair. ''Go ahead. Make all the threats you want. But if you think I'm afraid of you, you are very much mistaken.''

Melanie's smile was cool even though her blood boiled with rage. ''You should be afraid of me. If anything happens to Angel, you should be very afraid.''

''Why don't you just go away?'' Blanca said through clenched teeth. ''You don't belong here. There's no reason for you to stay now.''

Melanie straightened, her gaze searching Blanca's features. ''Is that why you got rid of Angel? So you could get rid of me, too?''

''Angel went home to her family. You should be happy about that.''

''It was Angel's family who came and got her?''

Blanca shrugged. "She will be taken to them."

"What's that supposed to mean?" When the woman didn't answer, Melanie said, "Oh, my God. It *wasn't* her family, was it. Someone else took her." A cold, dark fear washed over her. "Who took her, Blanca? Who did you let her go away with?"

Blanca lifted her chin in defiance. "He was a government official. He had the correct papers—"

"A government official?" Melanie repeated in disbelief. "How would a government official even know about Angel?"

Guilt flashed in the woman's eyes before she quickly glanced away. "There's nothing you can do about it now. Angel is gone. So why don't you just leave us in peace? No one wants you here."

Melanie leaned forward, once again flattening her palms on the desk. "You mean *you* don't want me here. What are you so afraid of? That I'll turn you in for treating rebel soldiers?" At Blanca's startled look, Melanie said, "That's right. I know all about it. And you know what? I don't care. I admire Dr. Wilder for not allowing politics to get in the way of his medicine. But when he finds out what you've done—"

"He won't find out."

Melanie's gaze narrowed. "I wouldn't be too sure about that."

"Oh, I'm sure. I'm very sure." Blanca's dark eyes

glittered dangerously. "Because if you tell him, you'll never see Angel again."

BY THE TIME Melanie arrived at the café late that afternoon, Angus Bond was already waiting for her. He had a table near the street and waved cheerily to her as she walked by. Minutes later, she joined him on the patio.

He rose as she approached and then when they were both seated, he motioned for the waitress. He ordered his usual gin and tonic, and Melanie asked for a pineapple juice.

"Is everything all right?" he asked worriedly as the drinks were placed before them. "You seem a little distracted."

Melanie toyed with her glass. "I'm fine. I'm just worried about a patient at the clinic."

"Anything I can do to help?"

"I'm afraid not. There's nothing I can do at the moment, either, so I suppose I should just try and put it out of my mind." *Until Dr. Wilder returns,* she silently added. Then all hell would break loose. Blanca seemed to forget that Melanie knew about the rebel soldiers they'd treated, and so had her own leverage. And she would use that leverage to find out where Angel had been taken.

"Can I ask you something, Melanie?" Bond's blue eyes regarded her with a curious gleam. "Why spend your vacation volunteering at a medical clinic when you could be off having some fun? You said you wanted to visit the Mayan ruins and the cloud forest. I'll bet you haven't done either."

"There's still time. And besides, I like working at the clinic. It's the nearest I can get to being a doctor."

Bond's brows rose in surprise. "You want to be a doctor?"

She shrugged. "I did."

"What happened, if you don't mind my asking?"

She tried not to sigh. "I lost my focus, I guess. I let things distract me."

He gave her a sympathetic smile. "You're young. You could still go to medical school if you wanted."

"Maybe. But sometimes I think it wasn't meant to be. If I'd wanted it badly enough, I wouldn't have given up on it so easily."

"We all make mistakes. God knows I've made my share." Bond picked up his drink. "Some are more obvious than others, of course. Alcoholism and addiction run in my family, but I'm not trying to make excuses for my weaknesses. One has to accept responsibilities for one's own actions. But I can only imagine what you must think of me."

"I'm not exactly in a position to throw stones," Melanie said softly. "I've battled a few demons myself."

"But you've conquered them."

"I don't know that you can ever really conquer them. You just try to keep them at bay one day at a time."

His smile seemed wistful. "You're obviously a very strong-willed young woman. I admire that."

"Don't," Melanie said with a grimace. "If I were

the kind of person you should admire, I'd be a doctor right now.''

He shook his head. ''I think you vastly underrate yourself, Melanie. And I suspect it's because you've had an unhappy life. For that, I'm truly sorry.''

Melanie's heart jumped at his words. ''Why should you be sorry?'' she asked slowly. ''You hardly know me.''

He paused, his gaze dropping. ''I'm sorry because there might have been a time when I could have helped you. But that time has passed. I see that now.''

Melanie leaned forward, the nerves in her stomach tightening at the little dance they seemed to be doing. ''Why do I keep getting the feeling you're trying to tell me something? Why won't you just say it?''

He suddenly looked indescribably sad. ''There's nothing to say.''

''Are you sure?'' she asked a little desperately.

He rose. ''I think it's best if I leave you now.''

''No, don't.'' Melanie stood, too, and reached for his arm. ''Don't go. Not yet. Please. If you have something to tell me, just say it.''

Gently he removed her hand from his arm. ''You came to Santa Elena looking for someone, didn't you?''

She nodded, her breath in her throat.

''I'm not that person, Melanie. I'm not the man you're looking for.''

He turned then and walked quickly across the terrace to the street. Melanie called out his name once, but he didn't turn, and for some reason, she didn't go after him.

I'm not that person, Melanie.

Then who was he? If he was nothing more than a stranger, why did he seem to know so much about her?

And if he was her father, why wouldn't he tell her? She'd given him every opportunity. She'd practically begged him to say it. But something had held him back.

Melanie caught one last glance of him as he hurried down the street. He walked with his head down, his shoulders stooped, as if he carried the weight of the world on his shoulders.

Whether he was her father or not, she couldn't help feeling compassion for Angus Bond, because she'd been where he was now.

When he disappeared around a corner, she turned away. But as her gaze shifted, she caught a glimpse of a man standing across the street in the shadow of a building. For a moment, something about him, the way he stood, made her think he was Lassiter, but she almost immediately realized her mistake.

It was the man she'd seen at breakfast the day before. The one who'd stared at her so strangely.

Melanie could feel his gaze on her now. He was watching her in a way that made gooseflesh prickle her bare arms.

Was that why Angus Bond had rushed away? Had he seen the stranger, too? Had he recognized him?

Unnerved by the man's surveillance, Melanie paid

for the drinks and hurried away from the café. Twice during her short walk back to the hotel, she glanced over her shoulder, but she didn't spot him again.

Once inside the lobby, she strode toward the elevator, anxious now to be back in her room. Not that her room was exactly a safe haven. But Lassiter had told her earlier that he would call her tonight. Or maybe even come by. And suddenly Melanie wanted more than anything to see him. To be in the security of his arms.

That stopped her for a moment.

Security in Lassiter's arms? Wasn't that a contradiction?

A hand fell on her shoulder, and Melanie turned with a start. She immediately jerked away when she saw who it was. The stranger who'd been staring at her.

He was tall, as tall as Lassiter, with broad shoulders and powerful-looking arms. He had dark hair, dark eyes. He was a very handsome man. Handsome…and dangerous.

"Why are you following me?" she demanded angrily.

"I'm not going to hurt you," he said in a voice as deep and dark as his eyes. "I just want to talk to you."

"If you don't get lost, I'll start screaming," Melanie warned. "Right after I rip out your heart with my bare hands."

Amusement gleamed in his eyes. "I believe you

would, too. But no need for violence. As I said, I don't mean you any harm.''

''Then what do you want?''

''Just to talk. Can we go somewhere private?''

''Sure,'' Melanie said. ''Why don't I just follow you down some dark alley?''

He grinned. ''Okay, someplace public, then. How about over there?'' He nodded to a table and chairs placed in an alcove off the lobby. ''Please,'' he said when she continued to resist. ''This won't take long.''

Melanie frowned. ''I don't even know who you are. So what could we possibly have to talk about?''

He hesitated for the space of a heartbeat. ''How about Jon Lassiter, for starters?''

She sucked in her breath. ''Who are you?''

''My name is Deacon Cage. Look, can we just sit down for a minute? This won't take long, I promise.''

Melanie didn't want to go with the man. Something about him made her distinctly uneasy. But the alcove, though designed for private conversation, was in full view of the lobby. Surely he wouldn't dare try anything with so many witnesses present. And God help him if he did. Melanie hadn't taken up kick boxing for nothing.

Reluctantly, she allowed him to lead her to the table and they both sat down. ''What do you know about Jon Lassiter?''

''I know that he survived a terrible accident,'' Cage said.

Melanie's stomach quivered. "How do you know that?"

"Because I was on that submarine with him."

She stared at him in shock.

"There were eight of us who survived," he said. "I've spent a lot of time trying to track all the others down."

"Why?"

"Because there are still a lot of unanswered questions about what happened to us. About our mission. No one seems to know why we were even on that sub. Our memories were erased, and I'd like to know why."

"And you think Lassiter knows more than you do? He doesn't."

Cage nodded, as if something she'd said proved a point. "He confided in you, didn't he?"

"I don't see how that's any of your business."

"If he confided in you, that means he trusts you."

Melanie glared at him. "Again, how is that any of your business?"

"Because I'm not just here to talk about Lassiter," Cage said. "I'm here because I think you can help us."

Melanie's suspicion deepened. "Us?"

"I represent a group of people who have a vested interest in the welfare of the survivors of that submarine."

"What group?"

"It's a little hard to explain."

"Maybe you'd better try," she said coolly.

He drew a breath as if not quite knowing where to start. "After we were rescued and resuscitated, we underwent intense mind control and brainwashing sessions to erase all memories of our mission and our training. But it went even further than that. We were also made to forget what they'd done to us at Montauk." A shadow flickered in his eyes. "They made us forget, but they couldn't deprogram what they'd taught us to do. Some of us have used those abilities for...well, let's just say, not for the good of humanity. Some of us have crossed over to the dark side."

Melanie felt hysterical laughter bubbling up inside her. "Do you have any idea how ridiculous that sounds?"

"About as ridiculous as your ability to walk through walls, I'd say. Or to phase yourself in and out of dimensions."

The desire to laugh faded, leaving Melanie with a deep chill. She didn't particularly like Deacon Cage, but she couldn't tear herself away from him, either. "I still don't know what you want from me."

"I told you. We want you to help us save Jon Lassiter."

She shook her head in confusion. "Save him from what?"

"From the dark side. From himself. Whatever you want to call it." Cage leaned toward her. "Whatever happened on that sub changed us. I'm not just talking about the brainwashing, the memory loss. I'm talking about a fundamental change in our souls. Lassiter walks a fine line.''

The look in his eyes turned Melanie's blood to ice. ''Even if that were true, how am I supposed to save him?''

''By giving him something to lose. You and Lassiter have a connection. Use it.''

Her heart started to pound in agitation. ''I don't know what you're talking about.''

''Yes, you do. Why do you think the two of you ended up here in Santa Elena? It can't be a coincidence, can it?''

He was asking the same question Melanie had been asking herself, but it frightened her to hear Deacon Cage say it. *He* frightened her.

''What do you remember about Montauk?'' he asked.

''Nothing.''

He peered into her eyes. ''Are you sure?''

She fought the instinct to shrink back from him. ''Of course I'm sure.'' But even as she voiced the denial, something strange seemed to be happening in her head. The noise of the lobby faded, Deacon Cage faded, and suddenly all Melanie could hear was the sound of sobbing. It was coming from somewhere nearby. It was coming from her.

She was in a cagelike enclosure where the two men who had kidnapped her from her backyard had brought her. She sat on the cold floor, knees drawn up to her chest, arms around her legs as she rocked back and forth.

"Hey, you okay?"

The voice came from the enclosure nearest to Melanie's. She lifted her head, and saw a boy of about ten gazing back at her. She could guess his age because he looked to be about the size of the kid who lived next door to her. That kid had just had his tenth birthday party in his backyard a few days ago, and Melanie had spied on him and his friends through the fence.

She wondered now if she would be home in time for her own birthday party. The thought of home, of her parents waiting for her there, made her cry even harder.

"What's your name?" the boy called softly.

She wiped her nose with the back of her hand. "M-Melanie."

"My name's Han Solo," he said proudly.

"That's not your name!"

"Sure, it is."

"You're silly," Melanie said.

"Maybe. And maybe I shouldn't be wasting my time with a pissy little kid like you, anyway."

Melanie was suddenly sorry she'd called him silly. She was sorry he'd moved so far back inside his enclosure that she could no longer see him.

She scooted close to the bars, peering into the shadows. "Are you still there?"

There was a long pause, and then a sullen voice said, "Of course, I'm still here. Not like I can exactly leave whenever I want."

"I have a cat named Daisy," she offered shyly.

"A cat, huh?" He moved back to the bars so that she could see him, although it was too dark for her to make out his features. "What color?"

"White."

"Black cats are better," he said.

Melanie didn't argue. After a little while, she said, "I'm cold."

"You'll get used to it."

"I want to go home."

"Who doesn't?" he said sagely.

"Where are we?"

"I don't know. Don't think about it. Just try to get some sleep."

"I'm too scared to sleep." She began to cry again.

"Here, take my hand." He stretched his arm through the bars toward her.

"W-why?"

"Just see if you can reach it."

Melanie put her arm through the bars, stretching as far as she could to touch him. When their fingers brushed, he closed his hand warmly over hers and didn't let go.

"Just hold on tight," he said. "As long as you can feel my hand, you'll be safe. I'll watch out for you while you sleep."

"Promise?"

"I swear."

Melanie's tears subsided, and after a few moments, she lay down on the floor and slept.

WHEN SHE AWOKE, the darkness disoriented her. She glanced around. There was a dresser. A desk. French doors through which moonlight glimmered.

She was back in her hotel room. But how? When?

Someone lay in bed beside her, and Melanie gasped, pulling the covers up over her naked body.

Lassiter rolled over and put an arm around her waist, trying to draw her to him. When she resisted, he murmured against her shoulder, "What's wrong?"

"What are you doing here?"

He opened his eyes. "What?"

She jerked the covers up to her neck. "You can't just phase into my room and crawl into my bed whenever you feel like it, you know."

He propped himself on his elbow. "What the hell are you talking about? I knocked on the door and you let me in."

"No, I didn't."

"Yes, you did."

She stared at him in confusion. "Then what are you still doing here? It must be late."

"I told you earlier. I'm not going back to the compound tonight. I've arranged with Kruger to be away for a couple of days. I'm here because I wanted to make sure you didn't have any more unwelcome visitors." When she didn't say anything, he frowned. "Are you okay?"

"I'm not sure. I feel kind of strange." She put a hand to her head. "I don't remember you coming to my room, Lassiter. I don't even remember how I got to my room."

"Next you'll be telling me you don't remember what we did here," he said in a voice that sent a tremor rippling along her nerve endings.

"You mean we—" She broke off as images flashed strobelike through her head. The two of them kneeling, naked, on her bed. Her back arched into his chest. His hands coming around to cup her breasts. His mouth on her neck. Something hard pressing between her legs…

"It's coming back to me now," she murmured.

"I should hope so."

She lay back against her pillow. "I had the weirdest dream just now."

"It must have been," Lassiter said dryly.

"I was down in the lobby when a stranger approached me. He said he needed to talk to me, but I don't think I dreamed that part."

Lassiter lay on his side, watching her. "What did he want?"

"His name was Deacon Cage, and he said he'd been on board the submarine with you. He said there were six other survivors besides you and him, and that he's been trying to track all of you down. He represents a group of people who have a vested interest in your welfare." She paused. "Stop staring at me like that. That's what he said."

"What did he want with you?"

"He said he needed my help."

"To do what?"

She slanted him a glance. "To help save you."

Lassiter's brows rose. "Save me from what?"

"The dark side," she said meekly.

He tried to keep a straight face. "Don't tell me. His name was Obi-Wan Kenobi, right?" At her blank look, he said, "*Star Wars?* Darth Vader? The Dark Side?"

"Funny you should mention *Star Wars* because there was a boy in my dream who called himself Han Solo."

"This just gets better and better." Lassiter rolled over and stared at the ceiling. "So how again is it that you're supposed to keep me from turning to the dark side?"

"By…" …*making you fall in love with me,* Melanie almost blurted. But for some reason, she couldn't say it aloud. She could hardly even bring herself to think it.

"By…?" he prompted.

"By using my womanly wiles, I suppose."

He gave her a look that made her heart start to pound. "I might not be opposed to that."

Melanie shivered at the deep, sexy timbre of his voice. "No? Not even if I were to…say…do this?" She trailed a finger down his flat stomach, feeling his muscles tighten as she continued a downward journey. "Any objections so far?"

He sucked in a breath. "Hell, no."

She found him, encircled him, and he groaned deeply as she moved over him, letting her lips follow her hand.

He plunged his hands into her hair. "Melanie…"

After a few moments, she lifted herself just enough

to settle over him, and then tightening her thighs against his hips, she began to move slowly. Very slowly. She had to. Because all it really took was for him to be inside her…

But it happened before she could stop it. Melanie began to shudder violently, and Lassiter drew her down against him, holding her close until it was over.

And then he took control…

THE PHONE WOKE Melanie. She had no idea what time it was, but when she reached across the bed to answer it, she realized that Lassiter had left while she'd been asleep.

Since he didn't have to worry about being missed from the compound, she had no idea where he'd gone. Anywhere, presumably, away from her. Spending a few hours in bed together was one thing, but waking up together in the morning…that was taking things just a little too far for a guy like him.

But as Melanie lifted the phone from the hook, the bathroom door opened and he stepped out, his dark hair glistening in the moonlight from the shower he'd just taken.

He walked naked to the bed, and for a moment, Melanie was distracted by the sight of him. Then slowly she lifted the phone to her ear.

"Hello?"

"Happy birthday, Melanie."

A tremor shot through her at the sound of her father's voice.

Chapter Thirteen

On the Pacific side of Cartéga, the cloud forest began at an elevation of about five thousand feet, cresting at the top of Las Montañas de las Hermanas Escondidas, the Hidden Sisters Mountains, at nearly six thousand feet, and then sloping down to the Atlantic at roughly forty-five hundred feet.

According to local legend, the mountains were named for an unusual formation at the summit— three women kneeling in a circle—but the sisters were rarely revealed through the veil of clouds that draped them.

As per her father's instructions the night before, Melanie and Lassiter headed north, toward the cloud-forest preserve where they would leave their vehicle and hike through the forest to El Puente de Sueños— one of the many suspension bridges that spanned a valley lush with orchids, mosses, ferns and bromeliads.

The road was terrible, little more than a goat track in places as it wound around breathtakingly beautiful lakes and waterfalls, then crept over bridges that placed them a hundred feet above the valley floor. At times it almost seemed as if they were driving in the treetops, and once, Melanie saw a pair of the elusive Quetzal birds land in a tree branch not twenty feet from the road, at almost eye level.

They were in Lassiter's jeep and had been driving with the top down until it started to rain. The higher the elevation, the cooler the temperature. Melanie was glad she'd worn jeans and a jacket. She'd seen tourists come back to the hotel from their tours in shorts and camisoles, remarking to each other how surprisingly cold the weather had been.

Lassiter wore camouflage pants and a dark green T-shirt that stretched tautly over his chest and shoulders, revealing the bulging muscles in his forearms as he drove. Dressed as *el guerrero del demonio,* he was one dangerously attractive man.

Melanie lay her head back against the seat and studied his profile as she flashed back to the shower that morning. He'd climbed in with her, surprising her, and then thrilling her as he'd pulled her against him, reaching around to smooth slick, soapy hands over her breasts, down her sides, reaching lower and lower until Melanie's legs began to tremble.

And then he'd turned her, lifted her, pressed her against the cool tile wall as he pushed inside her, making her cling to him in desperation.

Melanie's heart fluttered in excitement at the memory. It was amazing to her that after all the times they'd been together, she could still want him so badly.

She wanted him now. Her desire for him was like an obsession.

He turned to stare at her through his sunglasses. She couldn't see his eyes, but she knew they were dark, intense, smoldering.

Without a word, she unfastened her seat belt and leaned toward him. He cupped a hand around the back of her neck, drawing her to him for a kiss that was deeply thrilling and utterly devastating. Melanie slipped her hand up under his T-shirt, letting her palm ride over the hard muscles in his abdomen.

They hit a pothole and jerked apart while Lassiter struggled to get the vehicle back under control. "Maybe I'd better keep my eyes on the road and my hands on the wheel," he muttered.

"Maybe you'd better," Melanie agreed as she slid her hand inside his pants.

THEY LEFT the jeep at the entrance to the preserve and struck out on foot. Lassiter had strapped on a gun and holster. Slung over his shoulder was a rifle he'd grabbed from behind his seat.

They both knew full well they could be walking into a trap. Melanie had no proof that the man on the phone was her father, other than the fact that he'd asked her to meet him in the clouds.

But even though "touching the clouds" had been a secret between them, it wasn't much proof. Someone else could have read her father's letters and then arranged the meeting in order to lure her to a remote location.

For now, however, Melanie and Lassiter weren't alone in the preserve. They met several tourists hiking along the trails, and at one point, they stopped to watch a canopy tour traveling from one overhead platform to another, using zip lines, glides and rappels.

But once they left the preserve, they also left civilization. The rain forest became progressively denser and more beautiful. In any given spot, Melanie could see at least a dozen varieties of orchids, growing in profusion and rivaled in color and beauty only by the exotic birds that flitted through the trees.

"This place is incredible," she said breathlessly. "Like a paradise."

An unworldly noise exploded just over her head, and Melanie jumped, completely unnerved. "What the hell was that?"

"Howler monkeys." Lassiter pointed to the tree branches, and when Melanie glanced up, she had a brief glimpse of gleaming eyes staring back at her before they disappeared into the leaves.

It began to rain again after that, and Melanie was soon soaked to the skin and shivering. She'd worn a jacket but no rain gear, which was stupid, considering where they were. Lassiter was wet, too, but the cold didn't seem to bother him. Using a machete, he hacked a trail and set a pace that was difficult for Melanie to keep up with.

Finally they emerged from the forest into a clearing, and Melanie saw a footbridge just ahead. Unlike the newer suspension bridges in the preserve, El Puente de Sueños was a more primitive design, constructed of wooden planks tied together with hemp and nothing but rope handrails to hang on to. A hundred feet below, the valley floor was shrouded in mist.

"Bridge of Dreams," Melanie murmured. She turned to Lassiter. "Do we go across?"

"No. We find cover and wait."

He led her back into the forest to a spot where they could see the bridge, but were hidden from anyone approaching on either side.

Melanie found a damp log and sat. She could feel the moisture seeping through her jeans all the way to her underwear, which did not bode well for the trip home.

Meanwhile Lassiter prowled the perimeter of the clearing. He was in full demon-warrior mode, primed for battle. Jaw set. Eyes hard. Weapons locked and loaded. Melanie shivered as she watched him.

"Can I ask you something, Lassiter?"

He barely glanced at her. "Sure."

"What do you remember about your childhood? I know you said you were raised on a farm in Mississippi. Your father died when you were young, and you and your mother were close. But do you have specific memories? Like going to high school? Playing football? Do you remember your first car? Your first girl?" she added softly.

"I remember a girl," he said. "Her name was Sarah."

"Were you in love with her?"

"I don't know about being in love. But there were some pretty intense emotions, I think."

"Did you ever consider trying to contact her after you left the hospital?"

He shrugged. "I knew her a long time ago."

"You don't ever wonder what happened to her?"

"I don't even know if she was real, Melanie. So no. I don't spend a lot of time thinking about her."

There was an edge in his voice that didn't invite more questions, but Melanie had never been one to take a subtle hint. "Lassiter, what happens if my father does show up here today?"

He watched the bridge with a brooding frown. "We find out what he knows. That's the whole point, isn't it? To learn the truth?"

"I guess I'm asking about us," she said slowly. "What happens to us?"

He glanced over his shoulder with a scowl. "What are you getting at?"

"After today, there may not be much point in my staying on in Santa Elena."

He turned back to the bridge. "What do you expect me to say to that? Don't go? Move down here so we can keep right on doing what we're doing? I can't do that. How long would it take before that kind of arrangement wouldn't be enough for you?"

"Maybe you're the one who'd want more," she shot back. "Did you ever consider that?"

He faced her with grim resolve. "I don't think this is a good time to have this conversation, but you brought it up, so maybe we need to get a few things straight. I'm not looking for anything permanent here, Melanie. What we've got going…yeah, it's great. But when my job with Kruger is over, I'll be moving on to the next. And then the one after that, if I'm still alive. In my line of work, you don't think much about the future, and you sure as hell don't make promises you know you won't keep."

Melanie refused to feel disappointed even though she couldn't quite ignore the hollowness in her chest. "For someone who didn't want to talk about this, you sure have a hell of a lot to say on the subject."

"No commitments, no promises, no expectations. That's what we said. When it's over, it's over."

"So is it over, Lassiter? If my father shows up and we find out the truth, whatever that may be, is that it, then? I go back home and we never see each other again?"

When he didn't answer, Melanie got up and dusted off her damp seat. "I guess I'll have to take that silence as a yes."

He knelt suddenly as if he hadn't heard her, and lifted his binoculars to his eyes, using his forefinger to focus. "We've got movement."

Melanie tried valiantly not to feel hurt by his seeming lack of interest about whether or not he'd ever see her again because, after all, he was right. She'd gone into their…arrangement, as he called it, with her eyes wide open. No reason now to have regrets. She wasn't looking for anything permanent, either, because she'd learned a long time ago that today, the here and now, was all you could count on.

One day at a time, she reminded herself as she came up beside Lassiter. "What kind of movement?"

"Someone's coming out of the forest on the other side of the bridge."

Melanie's pulse quickened. "Can you see who it is?"

"Not yet. Wait a minute—"

"What? Do you recognize him?" she asked anxiously.

He handed her the binoculars without a word. She lifted the powerful lenses to her eyes and saw the man almost immediately. He was standing at the edge of the bridge, one hand on the rope rail as if ready to cross.

"Melanie?" he suddenly called. "Are you here?"

The sound traveled down into the valley and echoed back up to her. That voice—she'd heard it before. Last night on the phone. Years ago in her backyard. But it wasn't the voice she was accustomed to hearing when Angus Bond spoke. The Australian accent had vanished.

She lowered the binoculars, her heart pounding with an emotion she couldn't quite name. Elation? Fear? Anger? It was a mixture of all of them, she suspected.

"Melanie! If you can hear me, please say something. I've waited a long time for this moment."

She started to stand up, but Lassiter grabbed her arm and pulled her back down. "Not yet."

"Should I answer him?"

He hesitated, then nodded. "Go ahead."

"I'm over here!" she called.

"Is Lassiter with you?" Bond asked.

He nodded.

"Yes."

Bond waited a moment, then said, "Shall I come across?"

"Stay where you are," Lassiter answered, watching Bond through the binoculars. "We can hear you just fine."

"We need to talk, Melanie. I've got so much to explain."

Melanie rose. Lassiter tried to stop her again, but she shook off his arm. "Let me go. I have to do this. I came all the way down here to face him."

She walked out of the forest to the edge of the bridge and paused. Thirty feet of rope and wooden planks was all that stood between her and a man who could be her father. Between her and a lifetime of betrayal and loneliness. "If you're my father, why didn't you tell me yesterday? I gave you every chance."

"They were watching us. I couldn't tell you then." Bond spread his arms in supplication. "Please, Melanie. Just give me a chance to explain. Let me look into your eyes when I beg for your forgiveness."

He wasn't her father.

Melanie didn't know how she knew, but the revelation came to her suddenly, with a certainty that stiffened her spine and brought anger surging through her veins. "You're not my father."

He spread his arms again. "I am, Melanie. If you'll give me a chance, I can prove it."

"How?"

He put a foot on the bridge. "Just let me come across—"

Lassiter was suddenly at her side, rifle butt pressed to his shoulder as he stared down the barrel at Bond. "I said stay where you are."

Something changed in Bond then. The sorrow drained from his voice, leaving behind a quality that was cold and emotionless. And possibly deadly. "All right," he said with a shrug. "You're a very clever girl, Melanie, so let's just be straight with each other, shall we?"

"What do you want?" she asked angrily.

"I want you to come across the bridge and join me. In fact, I really must insist on it. We can either do it the easy way or we can do it the hard way. Your choice."

Lassiter's finger tightened on the trigger. "Or we can do it my way."

"It's not your decision to make, Lassiter. Melanie has to make the choice." Bond turned and said something over his shoulder, and instantly a young woman appeared out of the forest behind him. Melanie recognized her at once. It was Blanca. And the child she clung to was Angel.

The little girl tried to struggle free, but Blanca held her fast. Melanie could hear Angel's terrified sobs, and the sound tore at her heart.

Tears sprang to her eyes, and for a moment, her mind went back to the dream she'd had last night. To another terrified, sobbing little girl…

It hit Melanie then why she'd felt so close to Angel. Why she cared about this child more than any other. Melanie hadn't been able to save herself all those years ago, but she could save this little girl. She could save Angel. And in so doing, she might just be able to save herself.

"*Está bien,* Angel," she soothed. "*No tengas miedo.* I won't let them hurt you."

The little girl was crying hysterically now, but every now and then between sobs, she called out Melanie's name.

"Let her go, Bond," Melanie said desperately. "I'll do anything you ask." She moved toward the bridge.

Lassiter grabbed her arm. "What are you doing? That's exactly what they want."

"Don't listen to him, Melanie," Bond said. "If you come across, the child can go back with him. If not…she's coming with me."

Somehow Angel managed to tear herself free of Blanca's hold and like quicksilver, she darted onto the bridge, crying Melanie's name.

The suspension ropes swung crazily at the sudden movement, and Angel lost her balance as she was pitched from side to side. She was too small to reach the rope handrail, and Melanie watched in horror as she slipped over the edge. Dangling in midair and screaming in terror, the little girl clung to one of the wooden planks with her fingers.

Her heart in her throat, Melanie started across. Her every instinct told her to reach the child as quickly as she could, but the bridge swayed dangerously with every footstep. Every movement brought Angel closer to the brink.

Melanie was not halfway across when the ropes that bound together the planks beneath her feet snapped, and a section of the floor literally fell out from under her. She tumbled through the wood and ropes, frantically grasping for a handhold.

Like Angel, she managed to grab hold of the side. Her breath coming in painful gasps, she tried to pull herself up.

Lassiter was there in an instant, kneeling on the collapsing floorboards, unmindful of the danger to him as he reached down to grab her. His hands closed over hers, and he lifted her easily as she tried to fight off her panic.

But as he hauled her up, one of the suspension ropes snapped on their side of the bridge, and the floor dipped crazily.

Both of them grabbed for the rope handrail, but it came loose from the bridge and they were suddenly in a terrifying freefall. Melanie's first thought was of Angel. Oh, God, had she fallen, too? Even the part of the bridge that remained intact would have been swinging wildly when the support rope snapped.

Melanie hadn't even realized that she was still clutching the handrail until her and Lassiter's downward momentum was abruptly halted with a painful jerk. The rope had caught on something, and for the moment, they were left dangling ten feet or more from the bridge by only a thin strand of frayed roped that probably wouldn't hold their weight for more than a few seconds.

They were hanging face-to-face, and Melanie could see the grit and determination in Lassiter's eyes as he surveyed the situation.

"Lassiter…" she said breathlessly.

"Just hang on. Don't move."

Somewhere above her, she heard Angel cry her name again. She prayed the child was safe because she was in no position to help her at the moment.

The rope cut into her flesh where she gripped it so tightly. But she welcomed the pain. Pain meant she was still alive. And as long as she was alive, she still had a fighting chance. She'd been in tight places before and survived. She could do it again. They both could.

But the rope was giving way. She could feel it.

"Slide your hand up over mine, Melanie."

She glanced at Lassiter. His gaze was fixed on her, and something in his eyes…

Dear God…

Her heart started beating so hard she could scarcely breathe. She shook her head.

"Just do as I say," he said quietly.

"No! I can't."

"Yes, you can. It's the only way. The rope won't hold us both. Without me, you can climb back up."

Tears stung her eyes as a terrible pain stabbed her heart. "I won't let you do it. If one of us falls, we both do."

"That's not how it works." He slid his hand from underneath hers even as Melanie desperately tried to cling to him. But he was stronger than she was. And determined.

He hung by the rope now with one hand.

"Don't," she whispered. "Please don't do this."

He gazed into her eyes for the longest moment, and then he let go of the rope and plunged to the valley below without a sound.

MELANIE COULDN'T MOVE. It was all she could do to cling helplessly to the rope.

Lassiter was dead.

She squeezed her eyes closed, trying not to think about it. Trying not to remember the look on his face, that glimmer of emotion in his eyes before he let go.

In the moment right after he'd fallen, it would have been so easy to let go and follow him into the abyss. But even in her darkest moments of despair, Melanie had never been willing to give up on life. And she wouldn't do so now. She wouldn't let Lassiter's sacrifice be in vain.

But it hurt. And the pain would soon become unbearable if she gave in to it.

So she didn't give in to it. Instead, she summoned the memory of Lassiter's voice, and the sound of it in her head spurred her courage. *You can do it, Melanie. You're a survivor just like me.*

One inch at a time. That was how she would do it. That was how she would get to safety because that was how she lived her life. One step at a time. One day at a time...

The struggle to pull herself up put more pressure on the rope. Melanie could feel it giving, but she refused to look up or down. She thought about Angel and she just kept climbing, even when she could feel the stitches in her wrist also giving way.

And once she made it to what was left of the bridge, she hauled herself up, taking only a brief moment to draw in a gulp of air before she crawled across the tilting floorboards to safety.

Collapsing on the ground, Melanie buried her face in her arms. She had a feeling that at any moment, the shock and adrenaline would wear off and she would start screaming. She would start screaming and never be able to stop. But right now all she felt was numb. And that was a good thing because she still had to find Angel.

"Párate, ramera," a male voice said over her.

It was all she could do to lift her head. She found herself surrounded by half-a-dozen heavily armed soldiers.

One of them poked her with the barrel of his rifle. *"¡Apúrate!"*

Melanie dropped her head back in her arms, not even bothering to answer him.

"He said get up!"

Melanie knew that voice, too. She turned her head and watched as the crowd of men parted and Blanca stepped through. She was dressed like the others—boots, camouflage gear and the black beret of the rebel. She wore a gun strapped to her waist and a rifle slung over one shoulder.

Walking over to Melanie, she nudged her with her rifle. "If you don't get up, one of my men will shoot you where you are."

And if it wasn't for Angel, she just might let him, Melanie thought.

She struggled to her feet. "What do you want?"

Blanca gave her an insolent sneer. "From you? Nothing. I would just as soon put a bullet in you myself. But Señor Bond is not paying me to bring you in dead."

"Bring me in where?" Melanie forced the tremor from her voice. She wouldn't give Blanca the satisfaction. "Where's Angel?" she demanded. "Is she okay?"

"I told you before, the girl is not your concern."

"Where is she, dammit? Tell me—"

In the blink of an eye, Blanca whipped out her handgun and shoved the barrel underneath Melanie's chin. "You are in no position to make demands. I am in charge here."

And relishing every moment of it. Melanie's head was forced back, but her gaze never left Blanca's.

The woman's smile was deadly. "It would be so easy to kill you. And it would bring me nothing but pleasure. You and your kind make me sick. You come here to work in a Third World medical clinic so that you can go back home and have something to talk about at cocktail parties. So that you don't have to feel guilty about the decadent lifestyle you lead. You know nothing about my country. You know nothing about my people. And a week after you return home, you will care nothing about Angel. You won't even remember her.''

"That's enough moralizing for one day, I should think.'' Bond stepped through the circle of soldiers to walk over and calmly shove the gun away from Melanie. "You know the rules,'' he said to Blanca. "She's not to be harmed.''

Blanca gave him a look of pure hatred. "I'm a *capitana* in the People's Army. I suggest you show some respect.''

"And I suggest, *Captain,* that you show a little restraint.'' He turned back to Melanie. "Don't worry about the child. She's safe and no harm will come to her as long as you cooperate.''

Melanie gave him a look that rivaled Blanca's. "What do you want from me?''

"What do I want from you? I want your silence, Melanie. You've been asking far too many questions. Trying to uncover matters that must remain secret. Think of the problem as having a hole in a dam. There's just a trickle of water at first. Nothing to worry about. But one question leads to another. One memory prompts another, and soon the hole becomes bigger. Soon the water is rushing through so quickly the dam is in danger of collapsing. The only way to stop that from happening is to repair the hole before it's too late.''

He was talking about brainwashing. Reprogramming. Taking away her memories again. Nausea pooled in the pit of Melanie's stomach.

Bond gestured to the soldiers and two of them grabbed her while a third tied her hands behind her back. She winced as the rope came into contact with her newly opened cut. ''You need to come with me now,'' Bond said.

And the memory broke through the haze in her mind like a starburst. Suddenly Melanie knew exactly where she'd heard Bond's voice before. *You need to come with me now.*

In her mind, she saw him clearly as he walked across the backyard toward her swing. He was dressed in a long coat with a hat pulled down over his face.

She stared at him in horror. ''It was you. You're the one who took me that day.''

''See?'' He lifted his shoulders. ''Too many memories. Too many questions.''

A white-hot rage filled her. ''Where's my father?'' she screamed. ''What have you done to him?''

''Your father is dead, Melanie. He died a long time ago.''

Chapter Fourteen

A few minutes later, they emerged from the dense foliage onto a runway that had been hacked from the rain forest. A plane, engines revving, waited nearby.

In the few minutes it had taken to arrive at their destination, Melanie's shock had faded and grim reality set in. Lassiter was dead.

What was it he'd said to her earlier? When it was over, it was over.

But it shouldn't have ended like this. It shouldn't have ended at all. Because somehow, some way, Melanie couldn't let go of the notion that they were meant to be together. They'd been brought to Santa Elena for a reason.

And now Lassiter was dead.

Dead.

Tears stung her eyes, but she blinked them away. If she let herself cry, she wouldn't be able to stop, and she couldn't fall to pieces. Not yet. She had to find Angel and protect her from Bond.

He withdrew a thick packet of bills from his

pocket, and as he and Blanca stepped away from the others, two of the rebels grabbed Melanie's arms, dragged her over to the plane and shoved her inside. She saw Angel strapped to a stretcher at the back and tried to rush to her side, but navigating the close confines of the cabin with her hands bound was difficult.

Bond climbed into the plane behind her, and someone outside closed and locked the hatch. "The child is fine," he said as he took a seat. "She's been given a mild sedative to help her sleep during the flight. Now why don't you sit down and I'll help you with your seat belt? Once we're in the air, I'll untie your hands."

Melanie sat down because there was very little else she could do. "You got what you wanted. I'm coming with you. You don't need Angel. Let someone take her back to the clinic."

"I can't do that. As long as you're concerned for her safety, you'll be a lot more receptive to what we have to do. And besides," he added, "if you were to try and escape through a portal, you wouldn't be able to take her with you."

As the plane began to taxi, he reached over and fastened her seat belt. Melanie cringed away from him, then turned to stare out the window. As they lifted off the ground, she felt a terrible darkness descend on her.

Lassiter was dead. She couldn't get that last moment out of her mind. She couldn't forget what he had been willing to do to save her.

She tried to fight off her grief and isolation as she turned back to Bond. "Where are you taking us?"

"I think you know the answer to that, Melanie."

Montauk.

She closed her eyes.

"There's no need to be frightened," he said. "As I said, neither you nor the child will come to any harm as long as you cooperate."

"And I'm supposed to accept your word on that?"

"I'm afraid you must."

Her voice trembled with suppressed rage. "I find it a little hard to trust a murderer."

He lifted his brows. "Murderer?"

"Yes, murderer. You were responsible for my father's death, and maybe even my mother's. And now you've killed Lassiter. And I swear to God, I won't rest until I find a way to make you pay." She almost choked on the words, her chest was so constricted. She turned her head so that Bond wouldn't see the tears that were suddenly pouring down her face.

"You were in love with him," he said softly. "I guessed as much that day you came to the compound. But in a few days, your grief will be gone, Melanie. You won't even remember him."

She whipped her head around. "And that's supposed to be a comfort to me?"

He shrugged. "Maybe it would help you to know that I didn't have anything to do with the deaths of your parents. And I didn't cut the ropes on that bridge, either. I suspect Blanca may have had a hand in that."

"You're innocent of everything, I suppose," Melanie said contemptuously.

Silently, he reached over and loosened her ropes.

Pain shot up her arms as she stretched her muscles. When she brought her hands around to her lap, she saw that one of them was covered in blood.

"Here, let me take a look at that," Bond offered.

Melanie snatched her hand away. "I'd bleed to death before I'd let you touch me."

He withdrew a handkerchief from his pocket. "At least wrap it up. Here, take it," he urged.

Melanie hesitated, then snatched the handkerchief from his hand and wound it around her wrist.

"If you didn't kill my father, then what happened to him?"

"Your father was a very dangerous man."

"Dangerous to whom? You?"

"Dangerous to our government. Dangerous to the world. Dangerous to all of mankind."

She looked at him as if he was a lunatic. Which, she suspected, was not far off the mark. "What are you talking about?"

"Maybe I should start at the beginning," he said. "Your father was a brilliant quantum physicist. The work he did for us involved probability waves and the role of the conscious observer."

"Is that supposed to mean something to me?"

Bond merely smiled. "As far back as the early part of the twentieth century, subatomic experiments demonstrated that electrons have the intriguing ability to behave as both particle and wave. It was concluded by many that this duality, or the particle-wave paradox, was related to the observer. In other words, if the physicist conducting the experiment looked for a particle, he saw a particle. If he looked for a wave, he saw a wave pattern. It was therefore concluded that objects are not objects at all. They are only perceived as such when a conscious observer collapses the probability waves around them.''

''The Copenhagen Interpretation,'' Melanie said.

Bond lifted his brows in surprise. ''That's correct. The Copenhagen Interpretation has been challenged with some success over the years, but your father continued to believe and prove that there is an undeniable relationship between consciousness and the universe. With thought we are capable of experiencing our present reality, our past reality and our potential future reality. Unimpeded by space or time, thought opens the door to unlimited possibilities.''

''I guess I'm living proof of that, aren't I?'' she muttered. As Lassiter had been.

''You should be very grateful, Melanie. You've experienced what few people can even imagine. People would kill to have your ability.'' He leaned toward her, his eyes gleaming. ''You are one of the enlightened ones.''

''Forgive me if I don't feel particularly enlightened,'' she said. ''Most of the time, I feel like a freak.''

He frowned. ''Have you ever heard of the Illuminati? According to legend, they were an ancient people who achieved such a high level of mind expansion that time travel, interdimensional travel and even interplanetary travel were possible. But this stargate technology was lost when rationality became the central method of consciousness. Reason demanded proof. Therefore that which could be studied and quantified took precedence over the subjective.

"But we've entered a new millennium, and traditional sciences are in a state of flux, beleaguered by issues of objectivity, secondary properties and consciousness. The collapse of science as we know it is evidence that we're on the brink of a new worldview. Montauk is only the beginning of a new epoch, Melanie, one that will bring the birth of a new matrix and a new human. You, and the others who have been through Montauk, are the elders."

A thrill weaved up her spine, but whether it was dread or excitement, Melanie couldn't say. "That doesn't tell me what happened to my father."

"He began to have doubts about what we were doing, you see. To question the morality of playing God, as he put it. When he found out about the human experiments we were conducting, he threatened to go public with everything we'd discovered. We couldn't let that happen. Can you imagine the chaos it would have created? Mankind wasn't ready to accept what we'd discovered. There would have been mass panic. Economic collapses. Countries would have gone to war to obtain the secrets of Montauk. Secrets your father carried in his head."

"If you were afraid he'd go public, why didn't

you brainwash him? Why didn't you make him forget what he knew like you did with the others?''

''Because we needed him to finish his research. His work was at a critical stage. We had to find an incentive that would induce him to continue.''

''So you kidnapped me,'' Melanie said bitterly.

''Yes. We'd never used a test subject as young as you were at the time, and the possibilities—and problems—were intriguing. And you were amazing, Melanie. The speed with which you were able to accept altered states of consciousness and new realities was phenomenal. You didn't just accept them, you embraced them, so much so that we had to program limitations in order to keep track of you. Even Dr. Joseph Von Meter was impressed.''

''And my father knew about this?'' she asked in horror. ''He knew what you were doing to me?''

''He tried to stop it, but he couldn't. As long as we had you, he was completely under our control. And his work continued. But then one day, he disappeared. We sent teams of our soldiers all over the world looking for him, but somehow he always managed to elude them. We were worried about what he might do, with whom he might share our secrets. Desperate men do desperate things. But you were our ace in the hole, Melanie. As long as you were at Montauk, we didn't think your father would dare go public.''

''Then why did you release me?'' Melanie asked. ''Why did you take me back home?''

''Because after four years, we ran the risk of having your father conclude that he had nothing to lose by coming forward. So we sent you home to your mother because we knew there was nothing he wouldn't do to insure your continued freedom.''

The levels of manipulation were mind-boggling. And sickening. Melanie found she was trembling in outrage, for herself and for her father. ''You never saw him again?''

Bond shook his head. ''He changed his appearance, took on a new identity. We heard several times that a man matching his description had turned up in Cartéga. I used to go down there myself and search for him, but I never found him. It became almost an obsession with me.

''Then a few years ago, I found evidence in Santa Elena that he'd died of complications following emergency surgery. I tracked down the death certificate and even the doctor who'd treated him. But I didn't trust either one. I suspected his death was a hoax. So I kept going back, hoping that your father, if he was still alive, or Dr. Wilder would somehow tip their hand.''

''Dr. Wilder?''

''He's the one who treated your father. He was with Richard when he died. Wilder knew your father by another name, but on his deathbed, Richard confessed who he was. He said it was important for his real name to be used on the death certificate because someday, someone would come looking for him. And she would need to know what happened to him.''

She. Melanie's heart clutched at the thought of her father all alone in a strange land, unable to reach out to his wife and daughter even in his last hours.

"If you knew he was dead, why come back to Santa Elena now? It's been ten years."

"Because even after a decade, I still believed he was alive," Bond said. "When your mother died, I realized that it was the perfect time to draw him out. He knew you were all alone in the world. He knew you'd had an unhappy life. How would a father be able to resist reaching out to a daughter who obviously needed him so badly?"

"So you wrote that letter," Melanie said. "You made me think it was from my father."

"I took pains to make it look as if your mother had received it before she died. I felt it would be less suspicious if it appeared you'd come across it by accident. I hired on with Kruger so that my continued presence in Santa Elena wouldn't create suspicion. All I had to do then was wait."

"And in the meantime, you had me watched, I suppose."

"Yes. Your every movement since you left Montauk has been carefully monitored."

Melanie shuddered. "You had someone come into my room in Santa Elena and go through my things, didn't you."

"I had to be certain you hadn't somehow made contact with Richard without my knowing it. And now," he said, reaching in his pocket to withdraw a needle, "I believe you know everything."

Melanie shrank away from him.

Seeing the terror in her eyes, he said, ''Given your history, I can understand why you'd be afraid of having drugs in your system. But this is just a mild sedative to help you sleep.'' When she still resisted, he said, ''Don't fight it, Melanie. It will only make it more painful for you if you do. And for the child.''

MELANIE AWOKE groggy and disoriented. She had no idea where she was at first, but then, as the haze began to clear, memories came rushing back to her. Which was a relief until she thought about Lassiter.

No matter what Bond did to her, Melanie didn't think she would ever be able to forget Lassiter's face, the look in his eyes when he let go of the rope. He might not have loved her, but he'd willingly given his life for her.

But Melanie couldn't think about that now. There would be time enough later to grieve. A whole lifetime to wonder what might have been.

Right now she had to figure out a way to free herself, and then she had to find Angel.

She glanced around. She was lying on some sort of bed or examination table, but the room was so dark, she could tell very little about her surroundings. A red light blinked from a surveillance camera in one corner.

Lifting herself on her elbows, she tried to swing her legs over the side of the table, but she couldn't seem to make her limbs work. The drugs were still too strong in her system. A wave of dizziness swept over her, and she let her head fall back against the pillow. Gritting her teeth, she tried to summon her strength, tried to stave off the vertigo, but the pull was too great. Darkness descended again.

WHEN SHE OPENED her eyes a second time, Melanie had no idea how much time had passed. It could have been a minute or a week.

A figure stood over her, so dark she thought at first that it was nothing more than a shadow or a figment of her imagination. But then the shadow moved, like a panther.

Melanie tried to scream, but a hand clamped firmly over her mouth. "It's me," a voice whispered.

The drugs were still interfering with her reasoning. Melanie's mind was playing tricks on her because for a second, she thought...

"I'm going to take my hand away, okay? Don't make a sound."

She nodded her acquiescence, and the moment he removed his hand, she grabbed his arm, certain that he would dissolve into the darkness at first contact.

But beneath her hand was solid flesh. And then he bent over her and she could see his features.

"Oh, my God!" She put her hands on either side of his face. "How can you be here? I saw you fall. I thought you were dead..."

He put a fingertip to her lips to silence her. "I fell through a doorway," he said. "I'll tell you every-thing later, but right now we have to get out of here.

We're being watched. They'll be here soon, and I don't know how long I'll be able to hold them off.''

She noticed then that he was dressed all in black and was heavily armed. There was no question that he'd come to get her out or die trying.

"Lassiter, where are we?"

"Montauk Air Force Station. The place is mostly deserted now, but Bond still has a facility six stories below ground."

"Six stories…'' Melanie's chest tightened with claustrophobia. With panic. With a million suppressed memories. "How did you find me?"

He hesitated. "I convinced Blanca to cooperate."

Melanie shivered as she imagined just what it would have taken to gain the woman's cooperation.

"Can you walk?" he asked her.

"I think so." She swung her legs over the side of the bed, and he helped her off. She was shaky at first, but it only took her a moment to regain her equilibrium.

When Lassiter started toward the door, she grabbed his arm. "Lassiter, Bond has Angel. We can't leave without her."

"We'll just have to find her, then," he said grimly.

He walked over to the door and tried the knob. "It's locked. We'll have to go through."

Reluctantly, she nodded.

"It's the only way, Melanie."

"I know. It's okay."

"Are you sure?" Even in the dark, his eyes were so intense Melanie felt everything inside her quicken.

She'd thought never to see those eyes again. She'd thought never to have him look at her again the way he was looking at her now.

She wanted to throw herself into his arms, but there was no time for that. No time for anything but finding Angel and getting the hell out of there.

"When we go through," he said, "don't come back out. Not until I say so. They could be waiting for us right outside this door."

Melanie's heart started to pound at the implication. "But I have to come back out. I can't stay on the other side. It's too dangerous. Too unstable. The doorways will shift—"

"Just follow me. You can do it, Melanie. Trust me. It's the only way to get out of this place alive. Are you with me?"

She drew a long breath and nodded. Closing her eyes, she readied herself mentally and physically for the transformation. When she opened them, Lassiter was already going through. Without hesitation, Melanie followed him.

Immediately, she saw a doorway on the other side, and her first impulse was to use it. The urge was so strong, in fact, she actually started toward it. Then she paused.

And glanced around. Everything was very still and cold. Frozen in place.

She was strangely aware of the dimension she'd just left. She knew if she went through that doorway, she would find herself in the corridor just outside the room in which she'd awakened. And it was very possible that Bond would be waiting for her there just as Lassiter had said.

But if she went any farther, she might not find another way out. The dimensions could shift until the doorways were no longer aligned. She could become trapped, lost…

She couldn't see Lassiter, but she knew he was somewhere in front of her. Was he waiting for her? Or had he given up on her, gone on without her?

Suddenly, he appeared before her and held out his hand. Melanie closed her eyes and took it.

Immediately, she experienced a powerful rush of energy, an explosion of light and color, and then everything that had been frozen before now raced passed her in a blur. It was a sensation like nothing she'd ever felt before.

She was still cognizant of the other dimension and had an awareness of traversing long corridors, passing through rooms, down steep flights of stairs as they went deeper and deeper into the maze of the underground bunkers.

Melanie began to think that there really was no way out when a doorway glimmered just ahead, and somehow she knew that was where they needed to be.

She squeezed Lassiter's hand, and they stepped through into a large, dimly lit room with long rows of small enclosures fitted with metal bars.

A feeling of oppression descended on Melanie, and suddenly the walls started closing in on her. She put a hand to her chest, unable to get enough air.

"This is it," she whispered raggedly. "This is where they kept us. In cages. Like animals." She glanced up at Lassiter. "Do you remember being here?"

"No." His expression was dark and bleak as he gazed around the room. "But it doesn't matter anymore, does it? We're free now, and I intend to keep it that way. Let's find Angel and get the hell out."

"I have a feeling she's here." Melanie's hand was still at her throat. "This is where he would have brought her."

Halfway down the first row, Melanie paused again. She put out her hand to touch the metal bars on one of the cages, and a shock bolted through her body.

She jerked her hand away. "It's electric."

Lassiter touched a fingertip to the bar. "No, it's not."

Melanie stared at him in surprise. "You didn't feel anything when you touched that bar?"

"Nothing." He put his hands on her shoulders. "Are you okay?"

She stared at the enclosure as memories began to stir deep, deep in her subconscious. "I think this must have been where they kept me. That's why I had such a strong reaction to it." She nodded to the one next to hers. "There was a boy in that one. He used to hold my hand when I cried."

Lassiter took her hand and held it warmly in his. "Like this?"

And suddenly Melanie knew. Something awoke

inside her, a light dawning in a sea of darkness, and she stared up at Lassiter in wonder. "It was you."

He shook his head. "What are you talking about?"

"It was you, Lassiter. You were that boy. You took care of me. You held my hand while I slept. You tried to protect me..."

A powerful emotion swept over Melanie as their gazes connected. And then came a profound understanding. *You and Lassiter are connected. Use it.*

"We have to get going," he urged softly. "If we split up, we can cover more ground."

She nodded, reluctant to leave his side, but she knew he was right.

A few minutes later, Melanie located Angel. The little girl was curled in a ball on the floor, apparently sleeping. "Lassiter! Over here."

By the time he found her, Melanie had gone through the bars and was cradling the unconscious child in her arms. "She's alive, Lassiter, but her pulse is weak. We have to get her out of here."

He tried the door.

"It's no use," Melanie said. "It's locked, and it can only be opened with a code."

"And you can't come back through with her." Lassiter studied the lock. "Move back as far as you can. I'll have to blast it open."

Still cradling Angel in her arms, Melanie scrambled away from the door and covered the child's ears with her hands. She tried to protect her own hearing by putting her head between her knees. But when the shot came, the noise was excruciating. Angel roused groggily and whimpered.

"Es vale, el Angel," Melanie murmured. "I've come to take you home."

Lassiter flung open the door and swept Angel up with one arm as he gripped his rifle in the other. The sight of him took Melanie's breath away. But he no longer reminded her of *el guerrero del demonio*. He looked like a savior to her now.

They hurried up the aisle toward an exit, but before they could reach it, another door opened to their right. Lassiter spun, child in one arm, gun in the other, fully prepared to do battle.

When Hoyt Kruger stepped through, Melanie gasped in shock. She half expected Lassiter to open fire, but he stunned her by dropping his weapon to his side.

Kruger was also armed and also dressed in black. He motioned with the barrel of his rifle. "Come on," he said urgently. "I've found a way out of this place."

Melanie looked at Lassiter in utter confusion.

"Go," he said. And from his terse, one-word response, she concluded this was not the time to ask questions. Obviously, Kruger was there to help them.

They headed for the door, but as Kruger swung it open, they could hear footsteps pounding down the corridor. He slammed the door shut and pointed across the room. "Over there! Hurry!"

They raced toward the second exit, but Bond was suddenly standing in their way. Either he'd phased himself into the room, or he'd come in through another door that Melanie hadn't noticed.

He had a gun, but with Lassiter and Kruger flanking her, Melanie no longer feared him.

"It's too late," he said. "This room is surrounded. There's no way out."

"We'll see about that." Lassiter lifted his gun, but before he could pull the trigger, Kruger fired his own weapon.

Bond staggered back, clutching his chest, and then as he crumpled to the floor, a small army of grim-faced soldiers rushed through the doorway behind them.

Lassiter thrust Angel into Melanie's arms and gave her a shove. "Run!"

Kruger stepped over Bond's body and took the lead. Melanie and Angel followed at his heels, and Lassiter brought up the rear, running backward as he fired, buying them as much time as he could. They raced through corridors and up dark stairwells until Melanie had lost all sense of direction. And as they continued to run, Lassiter fell farther and farther behind.

Gunfire still ringing in her ears, Melanie followed Kruger up yet another set of stairs, and then, at the end of a long hallway, he burst through a door that led them out into a cool, moonless night. From the outside, the place looked like nothing more than what it was—a deserted airforce station. In the distance, Melanie could see the massive control towers silhouetted against a dark sky, and shivered, knowing she had seen them before. She had stood in this exact spot once before.

Her arms tightened around Angel. The child whimpered and clung to her.

A jeep came roaring up beside them. "It's okay," Kruger told her when she tried to back away. "He's one of us."

Melanie recognized the driver then. He was Kruger's partner, Martin Grace.

Kruger took Angel while Melanie climbed into the back, and then gently he placed the child back in her arms.

"We can't leave yet!" Melanie shouted. "We have to wait for Lassiter."

"Don't worry." Kruger turned back to the door. "We never leave a man behind."

But before he made it to the exit, Lassiter emerged from a doorway not ten feet away and sprinted for the jeep. Kruger jumped into the front seat, and Lassiter vaulted over the side into the back.

"Get us out of here, Marty," Kruger yelled over the sound of the engine. "Drive like the devil himself is behind us. And there's a good possibility he just might be."

Grace didn't have to be told twice. He hauled ass for the nearest gate, and as Melanie clung for dear life to Angel, Lassiter wrapped his arms around both of them.

Chapter Fifteen

They all returned to Cartéga that night aboard Kruger's private jet. But three days later, Melanie was back in New York.

Once the dust had settled, she'd quickly realized that there was no valid reason for her to stay on in Santa Elena. Her father was dead. There was no need to go on searching for him, and besides, Bond had told her everything.

There was no need, even, for her to remain for Angel's sake. Dr. Wilder had located the child's family in San Cristóbal where they'd fled after rebel forces had burned down their village. During the ensuing chaos, Angel had been separated from them. Someone had found her wandering along a roadside and realizing how sick she was, had left her at the clinic. Her family had been frantically trying to find her ever since, and now they had all been reunited.

Angel had been returned to her mother's loving arms. She didn't need Melanie. In fact, Dr. Wilder had tried to explain gently that her presence might even cause Angel greater confusion. So Melanie had bowed out of the child's life even though it had caused her great pain to do so.

And as for Lassiter…well, that was the hardest part of all. He'd been willing to give up his life for her—not once but twice. They'd been through hell together, but once they'd returned to Santa Elena that night, once she'd seen how quickly he reverted back to his demon warrior persona, she'd come to the painful conclusion that, in spite of everything that had happened, they were right back where they'd started.

There was no place in Lassiter's life for a relationship, and Melanie understood that. She'd known that all along. He was a mercenary, a soldier, *el guerrero del demonio.* And nothing in their past or their future would change that.

Melanie knew that the sooner she ended things with Lassiter, the better off she'd be. To prolong the inevitable would be to invite an even deeper and perhaps more lasting pain. She would get over this, she told herself. She would cut her losses now and move on before desperation or self-pity drove her down the path to self-destruction. Alone or not, she wasn't about to fall into that trap again.

So having resolved herself to the inevitable, Melanie was surprised, shocked even, to receive word that Hoyt Kruger wanted to meet with her in Houston. He'd even arranged to have his jet fly her down, and once she landed at the airport, a driver had been on hand to take her directly to Kruger's downtown office.

As the car sped along the freeway, Melanie kept asking herself what she was doing there. She barely knew Kruger. She couldn't, for the life of her, come up with any reasonable explanation for why he wanted to see her.

Lights winked on in the downtown high-rises as the car whisked her through the maze of one-way streets. The driver let her off in front of one of the more impressive buildings, and before she could change her mind about the meeting, a woman stepped outside and beckoned for Melanie to follow. She took her straight up to Kruger's office.

He stood with his back to the door, staring out the window at the Houston skyline, and Melanie knocked softly to draw his attention. He turned and greeted her, then strode over to his desk. He waited for her to be seated and then he took a seat, as well.

In spite of the spacious office, he was dressed much as he'd been the day she'd met him at his compound in Cartéga. Khaki pants and shirt with the sleeves rolled up past his elbows.

Melanie glanced around. The office was handsomely appointed with interesting artifacts and artwork, but there was not a single picture of Kruger's family.

"I suppose you're wondering why I asked you down here," he said.

"I'm a little curious," Melanie admitted.

"I have a proposition for you."

She frowned. "What kind of proposition?"

"We'll get to that." He sat back in his chair and regarded her for a long moment. "I think there are other things we need to discuss first."

"Such as?"

His gaze searched her face. "You might be interested to learn that I knew your father, Melanie."

She caught her breath. "When?"

"We met years ago, after he left Montauk. We were both working for an outfit in West Texas. That's how I got my start in the oil business. Have you ever been to West Texas?"

"I've never been anywhere in Texas except Houston."

He nodded. "It's a pretty bleak place out there. The last frontier, some call it. Not a bad spot for a man who needs to disappear."

"How long was he there?"

Kruger shrugged. "Not long. But bonds develop pretty fast in a place like that and they can sometimes last a lifetime. Your father came to trust me. Eventually, he opened up to me, told me everything. And in return, I made him a promise. If anything ever happened to him, I'd look after you."

Melanie gazed at him in astonishment. "Is that why you came to Montauk with Lassiter to rescue me?"

"I would have done that, anyway."

And somehow Melanie knew that was true. "If my father told you everything, then you must have known who Bond was when he came to work for you."

"Not at first. But I began to have my suspicions. That's why I hired Lassiter. I'd heard rumors about him. And after what your father told me, I had reason to believe those stories were true. If Lassiter could do what they said he could do, I thought he might be willing to help us."

Melanie thought about what Deacon Cage had told her that night. "It could have gone the other way, you know. He might have been willing to help Bond."

Kruger shook his head. "I pride myself on being able to sum a man up with just a handshake, and I knew after meeting Lassiter that he was someone we could trust."

"We?"

His gaze on her deepened. "I made that promise, you know."

"I won't hold you to it," Melanie said. "Because you probably took on a whole lot more than you bargained for."

"How so?"

"Just because Bond is dead doesn't mean the danger is over. Someone else will take his place. And I don't expect you to keep putting your life on the line for me. I don't want you to."

"Your father is the one they really wanted, Melanie. He was the real danger to them. Bond was a madman with an obsession, but the others…they won't risk exposing themselves as long as you don't become a threat.''

Her voice hardened. ''You mean as long as I keep silent.''

He leaned forward, his gaze on her very intense. ''What if you did go public with what you know? Who would even believe you?''

''When they see what I can do…''

''Is that really what you want? Do you think your life would ever be your own after that?''

''When has my life ever been my own, anyway?'' she asked bitterly. Her hands balled into fists at her sides. ''So I'm just supposed to forget what they did to me?''

''You could devote the rest of your life to finding a way to expose them. You could spend the rest of your life chasing shadows. But you'd always be looking over your shoulder. You'd always be wondering what waited for you around the next corner. You could let an obsession consume you as it did Angus Bond. Or, you know, you could get on with the rest of your life.''

Melanie gazed down at her hands.

''Which brings me back to my proposition,'' he said softly. He picked up a folder from his desk and handed it to her.

''What is it?''

''Take a look inside.''

She opened the folder and several brochures tumbled into her lap. The first one she picked up was from Baylor College of Medicine. She glanced up. "What's this?"

"Medical school," he said. "Are you interested?"

Everything inside Melanie went completely still. For the longest moment, she didn't even dare breathe. "I don't understand," she finally managed.

"I realize Baylor isn't the school you'd originally planned on, but it's an excellent facility and I do have a few strings I could pull down here. You'd be on your own after that, though. If you can't cut it…" He shrugged.

Melanie was too stunned to say anything for a moment. She bit her lip, not daring to believe that a dream could actually come true. "Why would you do this for me?"

"Because everybody deserves a second chance," he said quietly. "No one knows that better than I do."

Melanie still didn't know what to say. Could she really do this? Could it really still happen for her?

And who was she to even deserve such a chance?

She, who had so easily thrown away her dream the first time.

She, who had not even had the courage to face Lassiter before she'd gotten on that plane in Cartéga because she hadn't wanted to see the same look in his eyes that she'd seen in another man's eyes.

But Lassiter wasn't Andrew. And Melanie wasn't the same person who'd let a man's rejection devastate her. She was stronger than that now.

"I'll need some time to think about it," she murmured. But what was there to think about? She wanted this more than anything in the world. Well, almost more than anything.

"You'll have plenty of time to think about it on your flight to Cartéga," Kruger said.

Melanie glanced up in surprise. "Cartéga?"

"All the arrangements have been made, but you need to hurry." Kruger rose as if signaling that their meeting had come to an end. "The jet is refueled and waiting on the tarmac."

Melanie's heart threatened to beat its way out of her chest. She was going to Cartéga?

"I don't understand any of this," she said in confusion.

"It's simple, Melanie. You and Lassiter have some unfinished business."

"But…what about medical school?"

"What about it?"

"I thought—"

"Don't think," Kruger said. "Just go."

Melanie was backing toward the door. "What if he doesn't want to see me?"

"What if he does?"

"We had an agreement. When it's over, it's over."

"What if it's not over?"

"I can't just show up down there. What would I say to him?"

"You'll figure it out. Now go."

Melanie started for the door, then turned back. "I don't know how I'll ever be able to thank you. For everything."

"Seeing you look the way you look right now is all the thanks I need." He drew a breath. "You're an amazing young woman, Melanie. Your father would have been very proud of you."

Her gaze lifted to his and she saw it then, something warm and familiar in those vivid blue depths. Something she'd been searching for her whole life.

She took an involuntary step toward him, but something else in his eyes stopped her. A warning that reminded her as long as her father remained dead, she would be safe.

Tears sprang to her eyes. "I wish I could have told him how much I loved him," she whispered.

Kruger's eyes glistened with emotion. "He knew, Melanie. He knew."

THE TWO-HOUR FLIGHT from Houston to San Cristóbal passed in a blur for Melanie. There were so many things to think about. So many things to worry about—like the look on Lassiter's face when he saw her.

A car was waiting for her at the airport for the final leg to Santa Elena, and the driver's instructions were to take her all the way out to the compound. But Melanie asked to be dropped off at the hotel, instead. She needed some time before she saw Lassiter.

She still had no idea what she was going to say to him. Or what to expect from him. She wasn't even sure what *she* wanted from their relationship. Marriage? Kids? The whole nine yards in suburbia?

She still couldn't picture either of them leading that kind of life, but she was finding it more and more difficult to imagine her life without him.

HE CAME AWAKE suddenly.

A dark silhouette stood over his bed. In the split second before Lassiter recognized who it was, his instincts kicked in, and he slammed her down on the bed, trapping her between his knees.

Melanie's eyes blazed in outrage. "What the hell…?"

At the sound of her voice, he eased his hold, but he didn't release her. "I thought I told you not to sneak up on a man while he's sleeping."

"Yeah, but I've never been good with warnings."

She was dressed all in black, and even in the darkness, Lassiter could see her luscious curves beneath the skintight outfit, the rise and fall of her breasts.

His hands were on her before he could stop himself.

She grabbed his wrist. "What do you think you're doing?"

"Searching you for weapons," he said grimly.

"You think I'd come here armed? I'm not that stupid, Lassiter. I came here to talk to you."

"About what?"

She hesitated again, as if unsure why she was there. "I may be going to medical school. I thought you might like to know."

Medical school? It sure as hell hadn't taken her long to get on with the rest of her life. It had been, what? All of three days since she'd left Santa Elena. Left without a word, damn her.

Lassiter knew he should be happy for her, and a part of him was. He'd seen her with Angel. He knew that in spite of everything she'd been through—or maybe because of it—she was capable of great compassion. She had a gift that shouldn't be squandered. Certainly not on the likes of him.

But at the same time, he hadn't expected her to be quite so blasé about their parting.

"Congratulations," he said, and meant it.

"Thanks."

She licked her lips, and Lassiter thought she seemed a little nervous. Unusually reticent.

"There's another reason I came, Lassiter."

He felt his pulse quicken in spite of himself. "What?"

"I think we have some unfinished business, you and me."

He lifted a brow. "You could have fooled me. Leaving without saying goodbye pretty much said it all as far as I was concerned."

Melanie was amazed to hear an undercurrent of anger in his tone. And maybe even a little hurt. But then that would mean…

One step at a time, she reminded herself.

"I left without saying goodbye because I thought that was the way you wanted it. No strings, no commitments, no promises. When I asked you that day at the bridge what would happen to us once we learned the truth, do you remember what you said?

You said you weren't looking for anything permanent. When your job with Kruger was over, you'd be moving on to the next. And then the next. In your line of work, you don't think much about the future, and you sure as hell don't make promises you know you won't keep. Has anything changed since then?''

He ran a hand down his face as he glanced away. ''No.''

Melanie drew a deep breath. ''I didn't think so. And that's why I left when I did. I thought it would be better for both of us to make a clean break. Not allow things to linger. No messy goodbyes. When it's over, it's over, right?''

She could feel his eyes on her in the darkness. ''So why did you come back?''

''Because…it's not over for me, Lassiter.''

She could feel him pulling away from her, both physically and emotionally, and Melanie reached out to take his arm. ''I came back here to say some things to you that you probably don't want to hear. But I'm going to say them, anyway, because I don't want to look back a year from now, or five years from now, and wonder if I did the right thing. Regret is a terrible thing to have to live with, Lassiter.''

''Maybe. But there are worse.''

Melanie almost lost her courage at that, but she drew another breath to steady her resolve. ''The truth is, I care about you, Lassiter. And I think in your own way you care about me, too.''

When he tried to pull away again, her hand tightened on his arm. ''Just hear me out. And then if you still want to walk away, I won't try to stop you. I'll leave here and you'll never see me again. And maybe that would be for the best. Maybe we both have too much emotional baggage to ever get past it. We're both afraid of commitment, Lassiter, and it's hard for us to trust. But if we could someday phase through those walls we've erected around our emotions, we might just discover something wonderful.''

She could feel the muscles in his arm tense beneath her hand, but he didn't try to pull away this time. She took that as a promising sign.

''What I told you before about moving on to the next job, about not counting on the future. That hasn't changed.'' His voice was deep and ragged, as if he was trying to come to terms with something deeply painful to him. ''That's still what I do. That's still who I am.''

''I'm not asking you to change.''

''So what are you proposing?'' he asked almost angrily. ''That I drag you with me from jungle to jungle? From one hellhole to the next? Because, believe me, Melanie, these accommodations are luxurious compared to most of the places I've been.''

''You wouldn't have to drag me,'' she said. ''I'd be able to keep up and you know it.''

''What about medical school? I don't want you to give it up for me.''

''I don't intend to.''

''Then how would this thing ever work?'' he asked in exasperation. ''Even if I took a job with Kruger—''

"Whoa, whoa, back up," Melanie cut in. "What job?"

He shrugged. "An offer's been made, but I'm not saying I'm taking it."

"I understand." But Melanie's heart had begun to pound slowly, painfully.

"But even if I did, you'd be back in the States, and I'd still be down here. The logistics would work against us."

"Aren't you forgetting something, Lassiter? We're a little better at commuting than most people."

"You don't like to phase," he reminded her. "It's not natural."

"I could learn to like it. Besides, you're very good at it."

"It's not going to be that easy, and you know it."

"I never said it would be easy. But, Lassiter, I think we should at least try. You know there's something between us. Something special. Something real. Something that belongs just to us. Are we supposed to let it go without a fight?"

"You don't understand," he said in a strange voice.

"Then tell me."

He glanced away as if they were getting into territory he'd rather not explore. "I've done a lot of things in my life, Melanie. Experienced things most people couldn't begin to imagine. I've been in hand-to-hand combat situations. I've been trapped in a dead submarine hundreds of feet below the surface.

I've faced death more times than any man has a right to. But nothing has ever scared me the way you do.''

His words moved her deeply. ''Why would someone like you be afraid of me?''

''I answered that question once before, remember? I'm afraid of what I'd be willing to do to have you.''

She put a hand to his face. ''Haven't you been listening to a word I said? You already have me. You don't have to do anything except…kiss me.''

And he did. So gently it made Melanie want to weep. But the tenderness didn't surprise her. It had always been there.

Just hold on tight. As long as you can feel my hand, you'll be safe. I'll watch out for you while you sleep.

When Lassiter pulled away, he thumbed away a tear on her face. ''I've never seen you cry before.''

''A girl has a right to be emotional when she falls in love.''

''Falls in love…''

Melanie cupped his face and drew him back to her. ''It scares me, too, Lassiter. But we'll just take it one step at a time. One day at a time. Right now, you don't even have to think about it if you don't want to. For now, why don't you just take advantage of the situation? Enjoy the fringe benefits.''

''Which are?''

There was nothing gentle about the way Melanie kissed him, about the way she wrapped her arms and legs around him and pressed her body against his.

When he finally broke away this time, he was

breathing hard. Extremely turned on. "If you keep doing that, things could get wild around here. Someone might hear us."

"I don't care," she whispered against his lips. "I don't care, I don't care, I don't care."

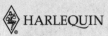

#741 A WARRIOR'S MISSION by Rita Herron
Colorado Confidential

When Colorado Confidential agent Night Walker arrived to investigate the Langworthy baby kidnapping, he discovered that the baby was *his*. A night of passion with Holly Langworthy months ago had left him a father, and now it was up to him to find his son—and win the heart of the woman he'd never forgotten.

#742 THE THIRD TWIN by Dani Sinclair
Heartskeep

Alexis Ryder's life was turned upside down the day she came home to find her father murdered, a briefcase full of money and a note revealing she was illegally adopted. Desperate to learn the truth, she had no choice but to team up with charming police officer Wyatt Crossley—the only man who seemed to have the answers she was seeking.

#743 UNDER SURVEILLANCE by Gayle Wilson
Phoenix Brotherhood

Phoenix Brotherhood operative John Edmonds was given one last case to prove himself to the agency: keep an eye on Kelly Lockett, the beautiful heir to her family's charitable foundation. But their mutual attraction was threatening his job—and might put her life in danger....

#744 MOUNTAIN SHERIFF by B.J. Daniels
Cascades Concealed

Journalist Charity Jenkins had been pursuing sexy sheriff Mitch Tanner since they were children. Trouble was, the man was a confirmed bachelor. But when strange things started happening to Charity and Mitch realized she might be in danger, he knew he had to protect her. Would he also find love where he least expected it?

#745 BOYS IN BLUE by Rebecca York (Ruth Glick writing as Rebecca York), Ann Voss Peterson and Patricia Rosemoor
Bachelors At Large

Three brothers' lives were changed forever when one of their own was arrested for murder. Now they had to unite to prove his innocence and discover the real killer...but they never thought they'd find *love*, as well!

#746 FOR THE SAKE OF THEIR BABY by Alice Sharpe

When her uncle's dead body was found in his mansion, Liz Chase's husband, Alex, took the rap for what he thought was a deliberate murder by his pregnant wife. But once he was released from prison, and discovered that his loving wife hadn't committed the crime, could they work together to find the *real* killer... and rekindle their relationship?

Visit us at www.eHarlequin.com

Harlequin Books presents the first title in Carly Phillips' sizzling *Simply* trilogy.

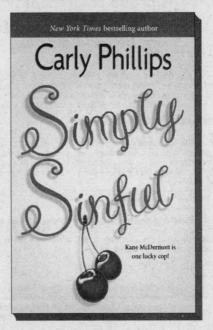

New York Times bestselling author

Carly Phillips

Simply Sinful

Kane McDermott is one lucky cop!

"Carly Phillips's stories are sexy and packed with fast-paced fun!"
—*New York Times* bestselling author Stella Cameron

Available in November 2003.

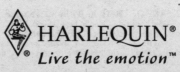

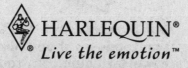

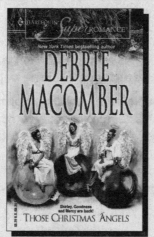

HARLEQUIN®
INTRIGUE®

Our unique brand of high-caliber romantic suspense just cannot be contained. And to meet our readers' demands, Harlequin Intrigue is expanding its publishing lineup to include **SIX** breathtaking titles every month!

Here's what we have in store for you:

❏ A trilogy of **Heartskeep** stories by Dani Sinclair

❏ More great **Bachelors at Large** books featuring sexy, single cops

❏ Plus outstanding contributions from your favorite Harlequin Intrigue authors, such as Amanda Stevens, B.J. Daniels and Gayle Wilson

MORE variety.
MORE pulse-pounding excitement.
MORE of your favorite authors and series.
Every month.

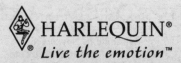

HARLEQUIN®
Live the emotion™

Visit us at www.tryIntrigue.com   HI4T06B

If you enjoyed what you just read,
then we've got an offer you can't resist!

Take 2 bestselling love stories FREE!

Plus get a FREE surprise gift!

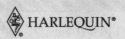
HARLEQUIN®

INTRIGUE®

Nestled deep in the Cascade Mountains of Oregon, the close-knit community of Timber Falls is visited by evil. Could one of their own be lurking in the shadows…?

CASCADES CONCEALED

B.J. Daniels

takes you on a journey to the remote Northwest in a new series of books far removed from the fancy big city. Here, folks are down-to-earth, but some have a tendency toward trouble when the rainy season comes…and it's about to start pouring!

Look for

MOUNTAIN SHERIFF
December 2003

and

DAY OF RECKONING
March 2004

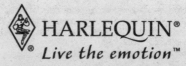
HARLEQUIN®
Live the emotion™

Visit us at www.eHarlequin.com

HICQMS